WITH MY L]

ROY FULLER was born in Failsworth, L٤
poetry at a young age, his first poem be
as a solicitor in 1933 and worked for many years at the Woolwich Equitable Building Society, ending his career as the head of the legal department. From 1941 to 1946 he served in the Royal Navy, becoming a lieutenant in 1944.

Though he wrote several well-received novels, Fuller was most famous as a poet, publishing his first collection in 1939 and many others over a more than fifty-year career. He also wrote several volumes of memoirs as well as books for children. He held the prestigious Professor of Poetry chair at Oxford and was awarded a C.B.E. and the Queen's Medal for Poetry in 1970 and the Cholmondeley Award from the Society of Authors in 1980. He was married to Kathleen Smith, and their son, John Fuller, is also a well-known poet and novelist. Roy Fuller died in 1991.

ROY FULLER

With My Little Eye

Who saw him die?
I, said the fly,
With my little eye,
I saw him die.

VALANCOURT BOOKS

With My Little Eye by Roy Fuller
First published in Great Britain by John Lehmann in 1948
First U. S. edition published by Macmillan in 1957
First Valancourt Books edition 2025

Copyright © 1948 by Roy Fuller

All rights reserved. In accordance with the U.S. Copyright Act of 1976, the copying, scanning, uploading, and/or electronic sharing of any part of this book without the permission of the publisher constitutes unlawful piracy and theft of the author's intellectual property. If you would like to use material from the book (other than for review purposes), prior written permission must be obtained by contacting the publisher.

The Valancourt Books name and logo are federally registered trademarks of Valancourt Books, LLC.

Published by Valancourt Books, Richmond, Virginia
http://www.valancourtbooks.com

ISBN 978-1-960241-39-9 (trade paperback)
Also available as an electronic book.

Cover by Roderick Brydon
Set in Dante MT

I WEDNESDAY, 5 *September*

As soon as I began to think of writing about what had happened I knew that I should have to kick off with a boring explanation. It would be pleasant to start with the astonishing thud of the pistol shot, but then the explanation would have to come in the middle of the excitement which would be even more boring.

I once heard my father saying of George Meredith that he put a barbed-wire fence (in the shape of a pompous first chapter) round all his novels. A fence, then, appears at the beginning of this narrative, but I hope that it will not enclose (as my father went on to remark) a field of cabbages run to seed.

My name is Frederick French. I live with my father in Chelsea, in a house which was built about the time George Meredith was born. A woman called Mrs MacBean keeps house for us (assisted by an ever-changing daily maid), and her husband, among other things, drives the car. A tom-cat called Melmoth is alleged to live with us also.

This, I know, is hardly a sufficient introduction to me, who plays a leading part in what follows. What colour of hair have you? Are you fat or thin? On Saturday afternoons do you play football or go for walks in the woods? What sort of books do you read? What sort of person is your best friend? Are you clever or stupid? How old are you? These are the kind of questions which readers like to ask about the heroes of books – and expect to find answered. But supposing I carefully described my appearance and my clothes and my habits and told you my age – do you think you would be much enlightened? The faces of boys are changing all the time; the clothes they wear are determined by their schools and their parents, and so, largely, are their activities. As for age, that is an absolutely unreliable guide to character. There is a boy at my own school, who cannot be more than eleven, with the wizened face and the deliberate gestures of a man of sixty. There is a boy of sixteen who has the red visage and cast of mind of an infant in arms. Do you see? And as I write this, after all that happened, it seems to me that during those six days I aged six years. At first everything was simple – including (by comparison) me – and then in the end everything was complicated. So if I told you my age it would mean no more than if I told you my size in collars.

Of course (you will say) French has given the game away already. Whatever the colour of his hair, it is worn rather long; he doesn't play football on Saturday afternoons; and he reads translations from the Russian. The way he writes – the very fact that he troubles to write at all – proclaims him to be a precocious highbrow. When he was ten he corrected his rich uncle's grammar; at twelve he spent his pocket money on concerts at the Wigmore Hall; at fourteen he contributed villanelles to the school magazine. His friends fear his bowling infinitely less than his tongue. Masters talk about him in the masters' common room. His father is glad when the holidays are over.

I should resent such an extreme view. I am both less and more complicated than that caricature, I think. Perhaps when you get to the end of this you will see clearly not only what I am like now but what I was like before it all started.

*

My father is Charles French, K.C., the County Court judge. What is that? some may ask, and I'm afraid that I must answer the question now. 'The whole of England and Wales (excluding the City of London),' says a useful but tedious manual I found in my father's library, 'is now divided into 411 areas or "districts", each with its own County Court.... A County Court judge must be a barrister of at least seven years' standing. He bears the title of "His Honour" prefixed to the word "Judge" before his name and is addressed in court as "Your Honour". He takes rank and precedence next after Knights Bachelor.... The County Court districts are grouped into fifty-nine circuits, each with one or two permanent judges. Each judge travels regularly round his particular circuit, holding a court in each district on days fixed and published at least three months previously.' And so on. My father's circuit is in some South London suburbs and a part of Kent. County Courts are not criminal courts. They don't deal with murder or arson or stealing, but with what are called 'civil' cases, where the amount of money involved is not large enough for the case to be heard in the High Court. They also deal with a lot of matters which by Act of Parliament have been specially given to them to deal with, such as claims by workmen, injured at their work, against their employers. They sound (and are) about the dullest places you can imagine.

However, during the holidays I sometimes go to court with my father to listen to the cases. Having a family interest in his court, I perhaps find it less dull than it is.

At breakfast on that Wednesday I said to him: 'Where are you sitting today?'

He peered over *The Times,* pulled his horn-rimmed spectacles from one eye and looked at me with it. 'I never start conversations in the morning before my second cup of coffee,' he said, severely. 'Why does it take you so long after you come home from school to remember the habits of civilization?'

This needed no reply, so to pass the time I took another piece of toast, spread butter and Oxford marmalade on it, and ate it, looking out of the window to where the rain was drenching the railings and trees in the square. After a while my father crumpled all the sheets of *The Times* together and let them fall on the floor.

'Heathstead,' he said, and lit a cigarette.

'I've never been to Heathstead,' I said. 'Can I come with you?'

'Certainly,' he said. 'It is an extraordinarily undistinguished list today. It will be good discipline for you. An exercise in the art of sitting still. Judgement Summonses this morning, applications, possession cases, and whatnots this afternoon. And please remember, if you sit where I can see you, not to yawn.'

'What is Heathstead like?' I asked.

'A decayed Victorian suburb,' he said. 'Like the rest of my circuit.'

'I don't think I want to hear the Judgement Summonses,' I

said. 'May I come with you, have a look round Heathstead, join you for lunch, and then listen to the possession cases?'

'Certainly,' he said, getting up from the table. 'But don't forget, when you are rollicking over the heath, that I am enduring the Judgement Summonses in order to keep you in toast and marmalade.'

MacBean brought the car round at ten o'clock and drove us to Heathstead. The court was a Gothic building in red brick near the station. Mr Wheeler, my father's clerk, a lean man with silver, brilliantined hair and a loose lower lip, was there waiting, and my father (though he is a small person) swept into the building with much dignity, with the policeman on duty at the side door saluting and a couple of court ushers seeing that his way was clear. MacBean drove the car away and I was left on the pavement with no responsibilities until one o'clock, at which hour my father had said he would adjourn the court for lunch. The rain had stopped.

At that time I had, of course, no idea how important Heathstead would become, and I wandered on the heath, very green against the grey sky, and over into the Park, and these places, though pleasant, did not seem at all significant. I must even have passed the end of Wren Road. Nothing of any interest happened that morning.

Nor was lunch very interesting. Instead of going to a hotel, the Registrar of the court took us to his home for boiled rubber chicken, and he and my father talked legal scandal until it was time to go back.

*

The courtroom was dark and hot. Very little light and no air came through the narrow, stained-glass, chapel-like windows which started high up the wall above the panelling. My father, in his wig and white bands and purple robes, sat on an ecclesiastical-looking chair behind a large desk on a dais. In front of him, on a lower level, sat the Registrar in a smaller wig, and the Registrar's clerk (who wore no wig at all). To their right was the witness box where plaintiffs and their witnesses gave evidence; on their left was an identical box for defendants. Between the boxes and stretching into the court was a large table covered with papers and books at which sat the solicitors appearing in the cases. At the back of the court and along the sides were seats for witnesses and spectators.

Everywhere was pretty crowded, particularly at the solicitors' table and round the witness boxes, where the lawyers and their clerks were moving about, and the parties in the cases were having a last whisper about them. I had found a seat behind the defendants' box, where, by leaning forward a little, I could see my father and by leaning back could yawn or pick my nose without being observed by him. I was full of the Registrar's boiled chicken and inclined to sleep. I thought my father seemed sleepy too; he put his chin on his hand and looked out into the courtroom, but since he had his reading glasses on I knew he could not see anything.

There was an application before the possession cases. A solicitor rose and said, 'May it please, your Honour.' 'Yes, Mr Kekewich?' said my father. Mr Kekewich was an extraordinary creature. His head was very large and his hair grew long to the very nape of his neck so that it looked like a lion's mane. His face was the face of a Roman bust, the chin small and receding, but the nose so powerful and the tiny mouth so strangely curved that there was no weakness in it. Mr Kekewich's appearance fascinated me to such an extent that I simply couldn't say what his application was about.

When it was over the Registrar's clerk stood up and called out 'Preece and Savage'. This was the name of the case that was to be heard next. Preece was the plaintiff, Savage was the defendant, and the reason for Preece bringing the case against Savage was this. Preece was the owner of a house, 2 Wren Road, and Savage was his tenant, the man to whom he had let it. Preece had served a Notice to Quit on Savage, but Savage had refused to leave the house. Well, one might think that the owner of a house could get it back from his tenant any time he wanted, but this is not so. A number of Acts of Parliament exist called the Rent and Mortgage Interest Restriction Acts. They started to be passed at the beginning of the 1914-18 war when building stopped and houses were scarce and the result of them is that owners of houses may not *(a)* raise the rents to more than a certain figure and *(b)* may not get the tenants out of them without getting the permission of a County Court judge.

All this has to be said, I fear. And a bit more besides. You see, it was not just a matter of Preece going to Heathstead County Court and asking my father if he could have his house back from Savage. The Rent Restriction Acts say that only in certain circumstances can the owner of a house turn his tenant out, and those circumstances have got to be proved. So Preece was there with witnesses to try to prove them and Savage was there to try to stop him proving them – because Savage had got a house he liked and had lived in for years and was paying a low rent, and goodness knows where he would find another if Preece succeeded in turning him out.

The Rent Restriction Acts are very complicated. The case opened with Preece's solicitor, a rather nervous young man called Sandys, standing up and saying to my father, 'I appear for the applicant, your Honour, and my friend Mr Brown appears for the defendant.' And then he launched out into a rambling explanation of how Savage became the tenant of 2 Wren Road and why Preece wanted him out, referring to sections of the Rent Restriction Acts and previous cases and trying to show that my father, according to law, ought to grant Preece's application for possession.

My brain whirled. My father had taken his chin off his hand and was leaning his head back against the worn crimson leather of the chair back. He seemed to be asleep, and no wonder. And then suddenly he cleared his throat very loudly and said in his flat, rather high voice:

'Mr Sandys, can we shorten this? What *precisely* are the grounds on which I can grant your client possession?'

Mr Sandys, who seemed to be in waters too deep for him, looked rather relieved. He picked up a book from the table and said, 'Paragraph *(h)*, Schedule 1, the Act of 1933, your Honour.'

'Very well,' said my father. 'Let us have the witnesses.'

Mr Sandys turned round to the seats behind him and motioned to a middle-aged man wearing a bow tie. This man got up and came into the witness box on my father's right hand

and was sworn. Mr Sandys scrabbled among his papers and then said:

'Is your name William Alfonso Preece?'

The man in the bow tie said yes, and then Mr Sandys drew from him the reasons why he wanted possession of 2 Wren Road. Preece was a married man with four youngish children, and a clerk in the accounts department of an engineering firm. At the beginning of the late war his department had been evacuated to the country and so had his children and he had, therefore, let his house to Savage. But a year and a half ago his department had returned to Heathstead and now he wanted the house to live in. At present, he had to live, with all his family, in two furnished rooms for which he was paying the exorbitant rent of £2 a week.

'Mr Preece,' interrupted my father, 'why have you waited for eighteen months before bringing this application?'

Preece turned deferentially to the Bench. He was a smooth character. 'I wrote to and saw Mr Savage many times, your Honour, before putting the matter in my solicitor's hands, because I hoped we could settle things between us without coming to court. All that took up a lot of time.'

My father sank back on his chair. Mr Sandys then asked Preece if Savage had any family.

'His wife is dead, I believe,' said Preece, 'and he has one daughter who has just left school.'

'Mr Sandys,' said my father, 'I think we might leave the defendant to tell us about that.'

'As your Honour pleases,' said Mr Sandys, servilely.

I must confess that my attention wandered after this. Savage's solicitor cross-examined Preece, but, of course, his story was true and unshakeable. It seemed to me that Preece had already won his case. Under the Rent Acts he had first to show that he wanted the house for his own occupation and secondly to convince my father that the court's discretion ought to be exercised in his favour. It was obvious that his hardship in the matter was very much greater than Savage's, and that my father would, therefore, make an Order that Preece should have possession.

It was stifling hot. I thought that a thunderstorm must be gathering because the Court seemed to be getting darker. The voices droned on. I thought about my return to school in a month's time and had a slight contraction of the bowels because I had not yet looked at the novel of Sir Walter Scott's, the reading of which had been set as a holiday task. This very night I must start reading it.

And then the thing happened that I can hardly plausibly explain. It seems to me that someone should have seen everything clearly, but no one apparently did. It was certainly very gloomy, there was a little mêlée round the solicitors' table in anticipation of the next case, and a great number of people behind the plaintiffs' witness box. But I still think it extraordinary that no one saw the whole thing. The evidence in Preece v. Savage had all been given. Mr Sandys was nervously doodling on his papers. Preece and Savage and their witnesses had dropped back into the anonymous audience in the court. My father had started giving his judgement.

*

It was the flash I saw first. And then the explosion cracked and echoed round the whole court. All was confusion. There were screams from women. My heart was pounding horribly. Someone shouted out 'Stop him!' I saw a humped-back figure move rapidly through the open folding doors at the back of the court. Everything had happened too suddenly for him to be intercepted, but several men, including an usher, ran out after him. I saw that people were crowding together on the other side of the solicitors' table, but what they were crowding for was hidden from me by the plaintiffs' witness box. I began to push my way towards them.

Through the hubbub I realized that my father was speaking. 'Poor Father,' I remember thinking. 'Surely he is not giving his judgement still.' But as I struggled through the people, entangling myself in the black gowns of solicitors I heard him say, 'The court will be adjourned for half an hour.'

Suddenly, alarmingly, terribly, I was on the front row of a circle of men standing round a body. The body lay on the scrubbed bare floor of the court. Its head was towards me so that I saw the face upside down, the hair forming, as it were, a beard, the brow a mouthless chin. Presented in this way the face was that of an ape, and unrecognizable. But as I looked at it a bubble of bright blood came from the mouth and spilled over the bow tie the body was wearing and I realized that it was Mr Preece. A man standing next to me said, 'He's gone.'

I felt someone at my elbow, tugging it, turned my eyes reluctantly, and saw Mr Wheeler, my father's clerk. 'His Honour wants you, Master Frederick,' he said, his lower lip very severe. He led me out of court, down some corridors, to a room where my father was sitting, still in his robes, but with his wig on the table beside him.

'So you found him,' said my father to Wheeler, rather obviously.

'On the front row,' replied Wheeler maliciously.

'One might have expected that,' said my father. 'A precocious child. Well, are you satisfied? Did you see plenty of blood?'

I would never have admitted it, but I was feeling sick.

Wheeler said: 'It *was* Preece sir. He's dead.'

'In that event,' said my father, fumbling under his robes for his cigarette-case, 'I shall have to adjourn the case *sine die*.'

Although I had seen everything, or as much as anyone had seen, I was bursting to ask a score of questions.

'How can you talk of the *case,* when the man has been shot dead?' I said.

'Something will have to be done about the case. It isn't over and the plaintiff is deceased. And, Wheeler,' added my father, 'find the learned Registrar and ask him if he can see me. We shall have to decide what to do about the rest of today's list. I suppose I shan't hear any more today. Goodness knows how I shall get through next week's list with this afternoon's added on to it. It is the old story, of course, not enough judges and a parsimonious government.'

'Father!'

'Yes, my child?' he said, exhaling a thin stream of smoke. Sometimes I believe him to be deliberately irritating; it is the approach of old age.

'What *exactly* happened?'

'I know no more than you. In order to read my notes I had my glasses on and that debars me from the long view.'

'Was it murder?'

'Who knows? It might have been suicide – a disappointed litigant. I don't think it is proper for me to say it, but my judgement was going to be in his favour. However, he may not have realized that and, impatient of the law's delays, shot himself. The Rent Restriction Acts have had less violent but not dissimilar effects before.'

'Oh, Father,' I said, 'didn't you see the hunchback?'

'The hunchback?'

'A hunchback ran out of court immediately after the shooting. Obviously there is no question of suicide – the hunchback was responsible. But I suppose it is possible that he was playing with the gun – cleaning it or something – and it went off and killed Preece accidentally.'

My father looked purposely bewildered. 'All this sounds ridiculously melodramatic. Where is the Registrar?'

Mr Wheeler came back with the Registrar a minute or two later. The Registrar was a stocky man who wore his wig half an inch above his beetle-brows, making him look like Caliban. He was obviously enjoying being in command of the situation.

'Mr Registrar,' said my father, 'I suppose I might as well disrobe.'

'I think so, your Honour,' said the Registrar in his bustling way. 'The police have arrived and I fear that the courtroom is given over entirely to their activities – flashlight photographs, foot-rules, heavy boots, and so on. The rest of the list, if you concur, your Honour, will have to stand over until tomorrow.'

'In that case,' said my father, 'Mr Wheeler will perhaps be good enough to telephone my house and tell MacBean that I shall not want the car at five o'clock. Frederick you and I will avail ourselves of the Southern Railway, and go and have tea at the Charing Cross Hotel.'

My stomach sank with disappointment. The Registrar cleared his throat meaningly. He said: 'There is just one thing, your Honour. The police have forbidden anyone to leave the precincts of this building until they have finished their enquiries.

Of course, your Honour, that would not apply to your Honour, but – '

'Mr Registrar,' cried my father, acting one of his parts, 'in this matter I am simply an ordinary citizen. An ordinary citizen.' And he began struggling with his robes. Mr Wheeler dashed forward to help him. 'Lie there, my art,' said my father, as Mr Wheeler at length draped the purple robes over a chair back. 'Now, I am at the disposal of the police.'

'Well,' said the Registrar, making little of all this, 'I certainly think the Inspector would like to see you.'

'An inspector!' said my father.

'Detective-Inspector Toller from Scotland Yard. He happened to be at the local police station on another matter when the call for the police came through from here. He obtained the necessary authority and is in charge of the investigation.'

'A very high-ranking police officer for a case of accidental death,' commented my father.

'Accidental death!' repeated the Registrar. 'What makes your Honour think that?'

'Frederick saw a hunchback cleaning a pistol and the thing went off by chance.'

'Father!' I protested. 'You are being very difficult. I saw nothing of the kind.'

'No, no,' the Registrar was booming emphatically. 'This is clearly murder. I will go and fetch Inspector Toller.'

I hugged my knee very hard with excitement, and tried to look unconcerned. My father's facetious mood had passed off and he was looking rather bored.

'Mr Wheeler,' he sighed, 'do you think you can manage to find a pot of tea? And a bun,' he added as Mr Wheeler went through the door.

*

The room we were in, like the courtroom, was panelled in what appeared to be treacle pudding, and was badly lit and a trifle suffocating. There was a bookcase, and a table covered with a piece of mauve felt, and two leather chairs round the empty fireplace in which there was an ancient fire screen pasted with cuttings from a Victorian scrapbook and heavily varnished. Flies hovered round the dusty light.

The Registrar soon came back with Inspector Toller. I don't know what sort of man I expected to see, but Toller's actual appearance gave me a slight shock. To begin with, he was vilely dressed. His navy suit with a white pinstripe looked as though it were lined with corrugated paper, and his white stiff collar had rounded points. Between the points was a small blue bow tie with white spots, whose neatness proclaimed it to be ready made up and attached by a stud. He had tried to disguise his policeman's feet with a pair of shoes pointed like destroyers out of which his bunions were almost bursting.

But it was his face I cared for least. He was fattish, and his face was fat, but the flesh under the skin seemed to have shrunk a little and the skin itself was pale with a yellow tinge. He looked like a once-handsome, once-jolly farmer who had just come out of jail with jaundice.

'Ah'm very pleased to meet you, your Honour,' he said in a vulgar Yorkshire voice when the Registrar introduced him. 'Ah'm afraid we've messed your calendar about.' But I shall not try to reproduce his accent; it should be remembered, though, that whenever he spoke it was in the flat Northern tones of a music-hall comedian.

When my father could get a word in edgeways, he said: 'Inspector, can you give me some idea of what all this is about?'

'No, your Honour,' said Toller, 'we don't know. The local station has nothing against the deceased. Perfectly respectable man. But we shall soon get to the bottom of it. Now, your Honour, out there everyone is being checked-up on. The solicitors are in their room and they're being checked-up on. I want statements from one or two folk who reliably saw something, and if your Honour doesn't mind I'll start on you.'

'It seems to me, Inspector,' said my father, 'that the use of this room might be a convenience to you. Subject to what you require of me, I shall only be using it long enough to have some tea.'

'I was about to suggest that to your Honour,' said the Registrar, not to be left out of things and frowning under his wig.

'Well, that's splendid,' said Toller, rubbing his great hands, and then calling out in a loud voice: 'Arthur!'

A tall young man with a very red face, wearing flannel trousers and a ginger jacket (who had clearly been standing just outside the door), came in in response to this call.

'Detective-Constable Jones,' explained Toller. 'Sit down, Arthur.'

Jones sat down by the side of the bookcase and took out a note-book and pencil. He was the shorthand writer. 'Now, your Honour,' said Toller.

'Inspector Toller,' said my father, 'first of all I must tell you that I observed nothing. I heard the shot, of course, and saw the commotion, whereupon I thought it proper to adjourn the court, but I have no useful information to give you.'

Toller had ensconced himself behind the table. He said: 'Does your Honour mind giving me some idea of what the case was about in which the deceased was concerned?'

'Not at all,' said my father. And very briefly, but beautifully clearly, he outlined the legal position which Preece and Savage had been in, why Preece had brought the action against Savage, and ended by saying that Preece had made out a case of greater hardship than Savage and would, if he had lived, have been entitled to an Order for possession of the house.

Toller sat there and took it in like a huge sponge. Just as my father was finishing, Wheeler came in with a tray on which there was an enormous teapot, half a dozen cups and saucers, and a plate piled high with glossy and somewhat dubious buns.

'I thought the Inspector might be here,' he said to my father, 'and that perhaps he would join you, sir.'

'Wheeler, you are invaluable,' said my father.

The Inspector rubbed his hands again. 'I can always do with a cup of tea,' he said. He ate almost all the buns, washing them down with sucked-up sips of tea that must have been scalding hot.

Wheeler said: 'I telephoned your house, sir, but MacBean had already left. He had some errands to perform on the way.'

'Well,' said my father, 'that being so, we had better wait here until he comes. That is if Frederick won't be too bored!' And he leered at me.

Not to be outdone, I said: 'Oh, I think I can stand it.'

'Inspector,' said my father, 'this is my son Frederick. I hope you don't think he is too young to hear all that is going on.'

'Pleased to meet you, Master Frederick,' said Toller, turning his little light-blue eyes on me. 'I'm sure he is the soul of discretion.'

Then, out of his full mouth, he asked my father a number of questions about Preece v. Savage. In the middle of this there was a knock at the door, and when my father called, 'Come in,' the long figure of Mr Brown, the solicitor who had appeared for Savage, entered the room. He was an elderly man with white hair fringing a startlingly pink skull. He had prominent teeth which made him talk with a lisp.

'Forgive me, your Honour,' he said, 'for disturbing you, but I was given to understand that the detective-inspector in charge of this investigation was here.'

'Come in, Mr Brown,' said my father. 'This is Inspector Toller.'

'Thank you, your Honour,' said Mr Brown, making a little bow as though he were addressing my father in court. 'Inspector, I hope I am not interrupting your activities here, but I felt I ought to come and tell you without any delay what I know about this affair. My name is Brown. I am the solicitor acting for Mr Savage, who was the defendant in the case brought here today by the deceased man, Preece. At this moment Mr Savage has a police constable at his elbow and feels very upset because it would seem that he is under some suspicion of having caused Preece's death.'

Here the Inspector shook his head.

'Well, whatever it is,' went on Mr Brown, 'there is the constable and my client is worried. Now this is what I have to tell you. Throughout the case (except when he was in the witness box) Mr Savage was seated immediately behind me, next to my clerk. At the moment the shot was fired it so happened that Mr Savage was leaning over to speak a word to me about a point in his Honour's judgement. It was absolutely impossible – and, of course, both I and my clerk are prepared to swear to it – at that moment for Mr Savage to have shot Mr Preece without us observing it. There is no doubt about this at all.'

'Thank you very much, Mr Brown,' said Toller. 'You did quite right, if I may say so, in coming to see me at once. I shall ensure that Mr Savage is allowed to leave whenever he wishes – and, naturally, without a bobby at his side.'

'My client will be very much relieved,' said Mr Brown. 'If I may say so, Inspector, you have taken a most reasonable attitude in this matter.'

'Not at all,' replied Toller, unctuously. 'We are here to serve the community and see that justice is done. I am only too glad to dismiss your client from the case.' And the Inspector got up and ushered Mr Brown fussily to the door.

'Good day to your Honour,' said Mr Brown, bobbing again.

'Good day,' said my father.

'I suppose you didn't see who *did* shoot the deceased,' the Inspector wistfully asked Mr Brown at the door.

'I saw nothing,' said Mr Brown.

'That's what they all say,' said Toller, looking round at us for his laugh. When Mr Brown had gone he said:

'Mr Brown is reliable, I suppose?'

The Registrar blew down his hairy nostrils: 'Partner in one of the best-known firms in the district. Mayor of the Borough in 1928. Won the M.C. in '17.'

Toller sighed. 'Well, it's not a case of the unsuccessful defendant knocking off the successful plaintiff. Didn't think it was, of course. But it has been known.' He went back to the table and, tipping back his head, poured the contents (leaves, I am sure, and all) of his tea-cup down his throat.

*

MacBean did not arrive with the car for another half an hour. During that time we (that is my father and I – Mr Wheeler had gone home and the Registrar had gone to his office) were privileged to hear Inspector Toller take a statement from one of the people who were in court at the time of the murder. This was no less a person than the dead man's wife, Mrs Preece. Toller did not seem to mind us being there – in fact, I think he liked an audience. I can hardly give an idea of the confidence he seemed to have in himself. My father told me afterwards that he was a policeman of great experience and had taken a chief part in one of the Trunk murders of some years back. Certainly he appeared to know all the moves in the game, and not only that, he appeared to be cocksure that by making the moves he would inevitably clear up the case. I did not think of it at the time, but the mechanics of that preliminary investigation – the examination of the body, the photographs, the fingerprints, the sifting of all the people in court – must have been done by the Divisional Inspector. Detective-Constable Jones was the only Scotland Yard man Toller had with him – he was not only a stenographer but also Toller's chauffeur and personal assistant.

Mrs Preece looked surprisingly old to be the mother of young children. She was a very pale thin little woman with bow legs, and feet that pointed outwards at angles of almost ninety degrees to her line of travel. She wore a dark felt hat the shape of a basin, very low on her face. But I shouldn't make fun of her. When she came in the room it was hard to tell what was upsetting her more – her husband's death or having to be interviewed by Toller in the presence of a judge. She was trembling, but her eyes were dry, and though she replied to Toller's questions in a faint voice, she at least replied. I had to admit that Toller handled her brilliantly. He was courteous, but it was only the courtesy of a new and very respectable lodger. And his northern accent became even more pronounced, conveying to Mrs Preece that they both came from the same social class and that she could, therefore, speak freely of everything.

Mrs Preece, Toller brought out, had been in court on Mr Sandys's advice in case it might be necessary for her to give evidence. She hadn't, in fact, given evidence. Those of her children who weren't at school were in a neighbour's care – the eliciting of this useless information was a typical part of Toller's tactics with her.

'Mrs Preece,' said the Inspector, 'now tell me this if you can. Just where were you when the' (Toller hesitated apologetically) 'shot was fired?'

Mrs Preece stared at the hideous fire-screen, from which she had never taken her eyes since she sat down. 'I was sitting near Mr Preece. He was standing up among the crowd round the witness stand. I heard the bang and saw him fall. Then I went up and saw him lying on the floor.'

Toller's head was slightly on one side with sympathy. 'Now were you sitting next to anyone you knew, Missis?'

'I didn't know anyone in that court, except Mr Preece. And Mr Sandys – but he was sitting with the other solicitors.'

'Was there anyone between you and Mr Preece, or had you a clear view of him?'

'No, I hadn't a very good view of him, but I could tell he was there.'

'Just about how far was he away?'

It was not until Toller had asked a number of questions like this that I realized what he was getting at. I glanced at my father in the shock of realization, but he was deep in a periodical called the *Law Quarterly Review* and apparently paying not the slightest attention to Toller's examination of Mrs Preece. So I turned back to look at Mrs Preece, with fresh eyes. In the way, I mean, Toller was looking at her – as a potential murderess. But I could see nothing beyond those absurd, pathetic Charlie Chaplin feet, and the passively suffering air with which she clearly accepted all the events of life – the furnished rooms at £2 a week, her four children, and now her husband shot dead among a lot of strangers and a cataclysmic fuss. I remembered what my father once told me when I was asking him about murder cases, that if a wife had been killed the police simply arrested the husband and vice versa and that they were usually right.

By the time I had thought thoroughly about all this Toller was on a different track.

'It's a terrible thing to have to ask you,' he said, with his bogus sincerity, 'but had Mr Preece any enemies?'

For the first time Mrs Preece looked disconcerted. Her eyes went from the fire-screen to the worn hand-bag which lay on her lap. 'Enemies,' she repeated.

'Anyone,' said Toller, persuasively, 'who wished Mr Preece ill. Any enemies at his work. Someone he knew who was mentally unbalanced.'

'Mad, do you mean, sir?' asked Mrs Preece.

'That way inclined,' said Toller.

'There *was* something strange,' said Mrs Preece.

Toller did not appear eager. 'Yes?' he said.

'There was some letters,' said Mrs Preece.

'Yes. I didn't understand them,' said Mrs Preece. 'Mr Preece didn't mean me to see them. I only found out about them by accident. My gas-lighter was broke. I was looking round for a piece of paper to light the stove from the pilot light on the geyser and picked one out of the bucket, among the rubbish. When I smoothed it out to make a spill I saw it was a kind of letter. Then later on I found another in Mr Preece's jacket pocket. I put that back.'

Toller was very casual. 'What happened to the first letter?'

'I kept it,' replied Mrs Preece. 'I couldn't understand it.'

'Where is it now?' asked Toller, patiently.

'Here,' said Mrs Preece, with dramatic effect. And she fumbled in her hand-bag, took out a purse, opened the purse, took out a piece of paper, folded very small, and handed it to the Inspector. Toller opened it out.

'*This is just another warning,*' he read aloud. '*You know what about. Lay off or you know what to expect. Elshie.* Do you know who Elshie is, Mrs Preece?'

'No. Mr Preece has a sister-in-law called Elsie, but she lives in Ireland.'

'And what did the other letter say?'

'It was something like this one,' said Mrs Preece. 'It was signed Elshie, too.'

'Were there any more letters?'

'Not that I saw.'

'What did Mr Preece say about these letters? Was he alarmed about them?'

'I don't know, sir. I never spoke to him about them. I knew he didn't mean me to see them.'

'Were *you* worried?'

'I don't know. I thought they was perhaps some joke.'

'Wouldn't Mr Preece have said if they had been a joke?'

'I expect so.' Then Mrs Preece added sadly. 'I thought too, that it might all be about some woman.'

Inspector Toller coughed and looked at my father as though

this was getting too adult for my innocent ears. But my father was still reading the *Law Quarterly*.

'Well, Mrs Preece,' said Toller, 'I think you must be getting weary of my questions. I know you're very upset and tired. Go home and have a good cup of tea. I'm afraid, you know, we shall have to have you for' (and again he made his little mock-tactful pause) 'the inquest. But we'll let you know about that later.'

As Mrs Preece left the room one of the court ushers came to say that MacBean had arrived. Toller interposed himself between us and the door to give my father a ceremonial farewell.

'We shall watch the newspapers with interest,' said my father, 'to see how the case ends, Inspector.'

'Thank you, sir,' said Toller, 'It has its points of interest.'

'Good afternoon, Inspector,' I said.

Toller turned benevolently to me and inclined his yellow face. 'Good afternoon, sir,' he said.

My father had trotted on ahead, following the usher. I said quickly to Toller: 'Was the gun found?'

Toller looked a bit surprised. 'Yes,' he said, 'on the floor of the court.'

'Who did it?'

'I don't know,' Toller said.

'Really?'

'Really.'

'What about Mrs Preece?'

'What about her?' Toller was amused.

'Is the hunchback known to the police?'

'May be,' said Toller. 'Are you interested in murders? Perhaps I ought to have taken a statement from you.'

'I didn't notice anything,' I said. 'Did anyone?'

'That remains to be seen,' said Toller.

I heard my father's voice in the distance petulantly requiring my presence. I flew. Toller called after me: 'Come to the inquest, young sir.'

*

That night was very hot. After dinner I sat in my bedroom with the window open. The trees in the square were still, patched a lurid green in the lamplight, and huge furred moths came in and battered themselves against the light. My father had dined at his club, so I had had my cold beef and salad alone.

I must confess that I had an attack of the horrors. I could not get out of my mind the visual image of that bubble of bright blood from the dying man's mouth and his upside-down face, and I had to pull my chair round so that I could see both the door and the window. I had not been so nervous since I read *Dracula*.

I could think of little else but the murder. It had for me two kinds of existence. First of all there was the mechanical side of it – what the doctor had said, what the witnesses had said, whether there were fingerprints on the revolver, what Toller really knew and thought about it all, whether the hunchback had been found, whether he had anything to do with it, and so on. About all that I had only the haziest conception. As a *case,* in fact, the Preece murder was far less clear, naturally, than it would have been in a novel or a newspaper. All the ends were untidy; there were great blanks in my knowledge.

But on the other hand the case in one sense was vividly real. The tones of Mrs Preece's voice, the appearance of Mr Brown, the personality of Inspector Toller, the gloom and the smell of the County Court, the crowd round the entrance as we went out – these things were a part of my life.

And now I must write down what was worrying me more than the grisly memory of the corpse. It had worried me all the time I had been listening to Toller. It was something that was little more than a hunch – something so vague that I could never tell anyone so official and matter-of-fact as Toller or my father. It was this. For some reason that I do not know, because I was not conscious either of seeing a suspicious movement or of hearing a sound from any particular place (though it might have been a subconscious perception of any of these things) – I was convinced that the shot had proceeded from a group of people round the plaintiff's witness box. That is to say, fairly near to where Preece had been standing when he had been killed. The group consisted of one or two solicitors and one or two other people. Of the group only one man was already known to me –

but the rest I am not sure I could recognize now. This man was the solicitor who had made the application to my father when the court had started its afternoon session: Kekewich.

Perhaps it was the name, or the massive head, or the Imperial profile – I haven't an idea; but that Kekewich fired the shot I was convinced. What could I have said to my father? All I managed to say, anyway, was (as we sat bouncing gently in the car on our way home):

'Is Mr Kekewich a good solicitor?'

'I haven't the least idea,' replied my father. 'He has never, so far as I know, appeared before me in the past.'

'But you knew his name.'

'The learned Registrar whispered it to me before he made his application. It is not judges but their clerks and registrars who are omniscient.' And he went on to criticize our lunch.

What could I have said to Toller? 'Watch Kekewich?' It was absurd. Toller called me 'young sir,' and for me his assumed attitude was one of mock seriousness. Clearly he had never himself been in his teens – or, indeed, any other age than a smug forty-five.

Kekewich. Kekewich. As I sat there, the only light the soft white glow from the table lamp, the name ceased for me to have a ridiculous sound, and took on alarming undertones of mystery and menace. Why should Kekewich kill Preece? And why so dangerously in court? Or was it dangerous in that crowded and gloomy place – did not the choice of venue for the murder reveal a bold and original mind? No one seemed to have seen more than I had seen: the act itself of murder had been done as safely as if the two protagonists had been alone on top of a mountain.

I got up and walked nervously through the empty corridors to the library, and there took down my father's copy of the *Law List*. I turned to the section which gave all the London solicitors and found the following entry:

'*Kekewich, Warren* (Apr. 1928), c.o. Bank-chas., Harbinger Vale, Heathstead.' The date was the date of his admission to practise as a solicitor (I discovered by turning to the key at the start of the list) and 'c.o.' meant, of course, Commissioner for Oaths.

I noted the address in my pocket diary, and then went back to my room. I now had two more sinister syllables. Warren Kekewich.

It was while I was waiting – quite illegally; I was supposed to go to bed at nine – for my father that I conceived the idea of keeping day by day the elaborate set of notes that have formed the basis of this narrative. Already, you see, I was determined not to lose my connexion with the murder. Already I saw my future profession, not as hitherto, that of a novelist of genius, but as private detective. Or perhaps the two combined. I went off into a foolish but stomach-warming day-dream. 'Not Mrs Preece, Toller,' I said, lolling back in my dressing-gown. 'Not even Kekewich.' 'Not even Kekewich?' repeated the Inspector. 'Then who on earth did it, Mr French?' 'It's quite obvious, Toller,' I said, toying with the man. 'Quite obvious. The murderer is none other than – ELSHIE.'

I woke with a start. I had really fallen asleep. My little dream remained vividly with me. Elshie. I had forgotten those curious letters Preece had received. Who the heck was Elshie? It was now after ten and I went along to the library again to see if my father had come back.

He was sitting in his usual arm-chair, lighting a last cigar, a book and a whisky-and-soda on the table at his side. He was not, naturally, awfully pleased to see me.

'Insomnia, Frederick?' he said.

'I'm sorry, Father. I fell asleep in my chair.'

'Over your holiday task I hope.'

'Not exactly,' I said.

'Have you started your holiday task?' he asked, meanly.

'I must confess not. I thought perhaps tomorrow.'

'Tomorrow and tomorrow and tomorrow.'

I changed the subject. 'Father, may I come with you to Heathstead tomorrow?'

'Certainly. But they will have taken the body away and scrubbed the floor.'

'Good lord, Father, it's not because of the murder. But I didn't hear much of the proceedings today. I thought I might do as I did today – a look round Heathstead in the morning and come to court in the afternoon.'

My father looked at me keenly and not without suspicion. 'Very well,' he said.

'Talking about the murder,' I said; 'whom do you think did it?'

'What a silly question,' said my father. 'Inspector Toller, of course.'

2 THURSDAY, *6 September*

Thursday started by being exactly like Wednesday, except that instead of rain there was sunshine. Before breakfast I had taken the precaution of writing two letters, the purpose of which will shortly be revealed. At breakfast my father read *The Times*. I ate my buttered eggs and thought about the case. In the revealing daylight my hunch about Kekewich no longer seemed probable. The murder seemed baffling and hazy, and I had the feeling that while I had slept Inspector Toller had solved the whole thing using conventional police methods. The morning newspaper had a vague account of the case – large headlines and no meat. I could hardly wait for MacBean to bring the car round. But subject to what I should learn at Heathstead I was determined to carry out the moves I had formulated. I thought how foolish my father would think me if he could see into my mind.

At Heathstead my father once again moved impressively into the court building. I followed him leisurely, looking for someone to question. I peeped into the Judge's Court: it was full of spectators (who hoped, no doubt, for another murder today). One of the court ushers was standing almost on the spot where Preece had been killed. I went up to him.

'Good morning, sir.' He recognized me, as I had hoped. He was a stout man with one of those noses which have the texture and something of the shape of a strawberry. I asked him if Toller was here today.

'Not yet, sir. But he'll be coming. He's taken over the witnesses' waiting-room for his inquiries headquarters. Couldn't remain in his Honour's room today, you see. He was here till nine o'clock last night. Very conscientious man, Inspector Toller.'

'Has he arrested anyone yet?'

'No, sir. Not yet,' he added with a meaning look.

'Do you mean he's about to arrest someone?' I was suddenly anxious about my own theories.

'Well,' said the usher, 'it's pretty generally known who did it.'

'Is it?'

The usher put his strawberry close to my ear. 'There's a law of slander, sir, but I know you won't let it go any further. The wife.'

'Really?' I was relieved. 'What was the motive?'

'Jealousy, of course. The deceased had been carrying on with another woman. Letters, there were.'

'And could Mrs Pre –'

'Sh,' said the usher hoarsely.

'Could the person you mentioned have shot straight enough? Handled the gun?'

'Lord bless you, they don't need no handling at that range. When I was in the Service, sir, I saw a new recruit what had never touched small arms in his life before blow the sergeant's hand off at ten yards . . .'

It was some minutes before I could get away. Before I went I asked him if he knew whether Mr Kekewich was in court that morning. He said, 'No.'

As I write down in cold blood this account of my movements at that time I am astonished at the lack of thought behind them. I cannot say whether I desired Kekewich to be in his office or not to be in his office, nor do I know whether if he had been in court and therefore not at his office it would have made any difference to my subsequent actions. And, more ridiculous still, I am not at all certain what I wanted or hoped to find out about him.

Anyway, I went straight from Court to Bank Chambers, Harbinger Vale. It was not far. On the way I took out one of the letters I had written before breakfast and gave it a last look over. It was headed with a false address and said:

Dear Mr Kekewich,

You have not acted for me before, but a friend of mine has recommended your name. I am sending this with my son and should be very glad if you will fix up with him a time to come and see me at the above address to write my will for me. I cannot come and see you because I am just getting over a stroke and also I am not able to write so my son is writing this for me. Hoping you can do this little job for me,

                         Yours respectively,
                         Henry Powder

Reading it again, I was still very pleased with this letter; it seemed to me that I had caught the genuine tone of a client simple enough to send his son to the lawyer's as to the grocer's, but yet with enough money to make it worth the lawyer's while to act. All this deceit made my heart beat quickly.

Bank Chambers were (as might be thought) some offices over a bank, approached by way of a small door at the side of the bank entrance and thence up a steep flight of stone steps. On the first floor was a firm called *The Rapid Typing Agency: Propr Miss Phippe*, and this was rather amazing, because if that firm could afford the first-floor suite of offices and Kekewich's couldn't, it made Kekewich a very small-time solicitor indeed. And I thought of his forceful appearance. On the second, which was also the top, floor was a small landing with three doors. One of them contained a panel of frosted glass on which was painted, *Kekewich & Co., Solicitors. Inquiries.* I had to take a few quick breaths before I could knock on this door and open it.

The room was very small. The door opened on to a counter, and behind the counter were two tables, with a typewriter on one of them and on the other some bundles of papers tied with pink tape and a copy of *Black Mask*. Between the tables was a dusty, old-fashioned, bedroom-type fireplace and on the shelf above it was a little mirror, a faded 1929 edition of Stone's *Justices' Manual*, a bottle containing an inch of milk and a drowned fly. A framed copy of a coloured caricature of the late Lord Birkenhead and a magazine clipping of Veronica Lake were on the wall.

Of the two people in the room, one was a fat girl in her twenties sitting at the typewriter, knitting away at a loose and pinkish piece of knitting, the other was a ginger-coloured boy not much older than I am whittling a groove in his table with such vigour that he threatened to cut it in half. Beyond looking up, neither of them took the slightest notice of me. After a long two minutes, during which I grew very red, the girl said: 'Go on, Arthur!'

The boy said: 'Go on yourself. It's your turn.'

'It's never my turn,' said the girl. 'It's not my job to attend to clients.'

'It's not my job to make tea,' said Arthur, waving his penknife, 'but I do it.'

'Oh, Arthur, you are awful. I'll tell Mr K, sure.'

'Tell him.'

The girl flounced about on her seat a bit and then, without putting down her knitting, turned to me and said: 'Yes?'

'Can I see Mr Kekewich?' I said.

'What name?'

'Powder.'

'Powder.'

The girl said: 'Mr Kekewich just went out. This minute.'

In spite of my resolute plan I was hugely relieved, and felt a sudden access of confidence.

'Oh dear,' I said. 'It's very important. When will he be back?'

'He'll not be back today. He's gone to Norwich.'

'Nottingham,' corrected Arthur, his back hunched with the effort of cutting.

'Norwich. He told me himself.'

'He told me Nottingham when I took him the *ABC*. You ought to clean your ears out.'

The girl said to me very distinctly: 'Mr Kekewich has gone to Norwich.'

Arthur laughed derisively.

But while this cross-talk was going on I had noticed on the counter, lying on top of a volume of the *London Telephone Directory*, the *ABC Railway Guide*. Sticking out of its last few pages was an envelope as a marker.

'Would you like to leave a message?' asked the girl.

'I'd rather leave a note, if you don't mind.'

'I don't mind.'

'I wonder if you could give me a piece of paper?'

The girl passed one up from her table. With it I carefully covered the *ABC* and, leaning my arm round it, started to write.

But, as it turned out, there was no need to go to such lengths; Arthur and the girl started into an argument again and took no more notice of me. I was easily able to open the *ABC* at the page marked by the envelope without being observed. What it showed was neither Norwich nor Nottingham, but the service between Charing Cross and Westsea.

Of course, it was a slim chance – not only that Kekewich was, in fact, going to Westsea, but also that his journey had any connexion with the murder. But that morning I was in a fever of detectivitis and willing to take any chance so long as I *did* something other than go back and sit in court or go home and read at my holiday task. On my piece of paper I wrote the first of my forged letters, but omitted the bogus address in case Kekewich afterwards became suspicious and investigated it. I asked the girl for an envelope which she ungraciously gave me. Arthur began to look at me with slight curiosity. I put my note in the envelope, sealed it, wrote *Warren Kekewich Esq.* on the outside and then could not resist saying: 'Which of you is prepared to give this to Mr Kekewich?' Arthur's mouth dropped slightly, and the girl said: 'What a cheek!' but neither moved, and so I left the envelope on the counter and went out.

I flew down the stairs and along Harbinger Vale to the court. In a sort of yard at the back I found my friend, the bottle-nosed usher, having a surreptitious smoke.

'Can't go a whole morning without a drag, sir,' he said apologetically, showing a cigarette in his great hand, the lighted end towards the palm. 'Have one?'

'I don't smoke within one mile of my father.'

'Quite right. I used to suck rose-bud cachous when I was a lad,' he said, reminiscently.

I cut him short. 'Would you mind giving this note to my father when he adjourns at lunch-time?'

He said that he'd be pleased to, so I handed him the second of the letters I had written before breakfast, prepared for just such an emergency as this. It said:

My dear father,
I've met Ronnie Reeves – you remember, the boy at school

who put a dead rabbit in one of the lavatory cisterns. He lives at Chislehurst and has asked me to go to lunch. Hope this is all right. I'll be home for dinner. Sorry to miss court.

Love,
Frederick

Kekewich was not on the platform at Heathstead, but I hardly expected him to be. The service to Charing Cross was frequent, and I was up there in twenty minutes. I was aiming for the eleven fifty-five train to Westsea and hoped that Kekewich was aiming likewise.

Charing Cross station seemed curiously crowded. There were a great many people at the bookstall and round the entrance to Number 6 Platform, and I had to queue to get a ticket. That slow progress to the booking office ground the skin off my nerves. I fidgeted and counted my money and scanned the passers-by and read thirty times the sale bill of a block of freehold ground rents in Deptford. When I emerged into the main part of the station again I saw the reason for the congestion written up on a blackboard. WESTSEA RACES. EXTRA TRAINS WILL RUN TODAY FROM THIS STATION AS FOLLOWS. Then it gave a list of trains at about fifteen-minute intervals from half past eleven.

When I saw this notice I looked round guiltily as though my father might be watching my folly. All was explained. Kekewich was having a day at the races and had been too weak-minded to tell either of his clerks the truth. Not perhaps weak-minded; it would not do, I supposed, for solicitors to be known as racegoers. And what train was he going by? I stood in a whirl, with people whizzing round me.

And then I saw, coming up the steps from the underground lavatory, Kekewich. He was not a tall man, but his face stood out from all the others like a joker in a hand of cards. On top of that strange hair, which was neither blond nor grey, he was wearing a smallish bowler hat; underneath the hat was the pale, degenerate, Roman countenance, incongruously smoking a cigar. He carried a dispatch case and a newspaper. At the sight of him half my doubts vanished. I became Hawkshaw the detective again and wormed after him through the crowd.

He went straight on to the platform for the Westsea train, and there I lost him. People were four deep along the edge of the platform, waiting for the train to come in. When it came I had to dash for the nearest compartment without locating Kekewich. I was frightened of being left behind.

It was a grim journey. I had a seat beside a man who drank bottled beer almost continuously and opposite another who ate pies. The sun poured on me through the coiled grey haze of cigarette smoke. There was a continual rustle of newspapers as everyone looked at the racing programme and read the tipsters. The names of dozens of horses reverberated in my brain – Lunacharski, Mask of Anarchy, Thermidor, Molly Bloom, Armadale, The Alchemist, Irene, and Libido – all these, and more, were certain winners according to the men in the carriage. But the train was fast and ran to Westsea without stopping, and soon I was in the fresh air, looking round, bewilderedly I imagine, for Kekewich.

I did not see him until I had struggled out of the station. A sea breeze was blowing. Vendors of race-cards stood on the pavement and shouted. Two men were in the gutter playing *The Entry of the Gladiators* on cornet and concertina. Taxis and cars were lined up, their drivers calling 'Ten bob to the course.' The bowler hat and the Imperial profile vanished into an antique Austin and was driven off. I couldn't afford ten shillings, so I stood wondering what to do. At last I asked someone how far it was to the racecourse, was told twenty minutes' walk, and set off, following the crowd. It was all uphill. After ten minutes I could see Westsea spread out below in a gentle arc along the wrinkled water, and the pier, and a boat with a brown smudge of smoke. In front rose a distant green hump of the downs, scarred with chalk. The sky was blue, with complicated white clouds blossoming from the horizon.

It was a hot and exhausting walk and took at least thirty-five minutes. After it, I was in no fit state to grapple with the ambiguities of getting in the race-course. It was all much less simple than I had pictured. There were various prices of admission to various parts of the course – Grand Stand, Silver Ring, and so on. And then, when I looked at my money, I found I had only eight and seven pence. It was essential to keep something in reserve if

I was to go on tracking Kekewich, so after some indecision I paid three shillings and went into the cheapest part, which was just called 'the Course'. I did not expect to find Kekewich there, but imagined I might be able to watch him from afar as he sat in the lordly stand.

Vain imagination! The stand was about half a mile away from the enclosure to which my three shillings had admitted me, and whatever sinister activity Kekewich might be pursuing there would remain for ever unknown to me. Unless I could come by some more money and get into the stand. It was not for some minutes (as I wandered rather aimlessly about on the short, parched grass – already starting to be littered with empty cigarette packets and pie crusts, and kept an eye open for Kekewich on the off chance) that I realized I was in the very place for making money.

Near the white rails which divided the enclosure from the race-track itself were the bookmakers. Some were under umbrellas, some stood on little wooden dais; all had boards on which were written the names of the horses running in the first race, and against each name the odds against the horse winning which the bookmaker was prepared to give. On these boards or on others were the names of the bookmakers, such as JOE CAPE OF BRIXTON. AT ALL JOCKEY CLUB AND N.H. MEETINGS and TOMMY FELDMAN, BRIGHTON. THE OLD FIRM. A confused and hoarse shouting came from these men.

The first thing to do, I realized, was to buy a race-card and find out the names of the runners and the jockeys. I tried to remember all I had ever heard about horse-racing. MacBean was a man who often betted – the milkman took his bets, I believe. 'I always go for the favourite in the first race,' I had heard him say. Or was it, 'I *never* go for the favourite in the first race'? 'Follow Gordon Richards at Bath,' I was certain he used to say, too. But, alas, this was not Bath but Westsea. I bought a race-card for sixpence.

It was a mine of information. Each horse's owner, trainer, father, mother, number, weight to be carried, name of jockey, the colours he was wearing, were listed – to study the thing properly was a holiday task. I turned to the first race, which was called a Selling Plate, run over five furlongs, and to start at two-thirty.

The time was now two-ten. I found a fairly quiet place near a tent where they were selling refreshments and, resisting a temptation to spend money on a bottle of lemonade, sat down on the grass.

There were nine horses in the race. When I had read all about them, two of them stuck out in my mind. One was Irene, which I had heard mentioned in the train. The other was a horse called Murder Most Foul; if life held any coincidences, that horse must win. I got up and went towards the row of bookmakers. I had to pass a group of people standing round a sharp-featured man wearing a bowler hat on which was painted in white the one word 'Billy'. This man was shuffling in his hands a stack of little envelopes and saying in a penetrating voice, 'Yes, it's Billy. It's Billy. It's Billy. It's your Newmarket man. It's Billy, the man from Newmarket. I've got something. I've got something. I've got something for this afternoon. You won't find it in no newspaper. No, you won't find it there. There's no one else giving this one. This is a hot one. This is hot, this one. Only Billy knows about this one. Billy from Newmarket. Billy's here. Billy's here. And he's got a winner. He's got a winner for this afternoon. It won't start at no evens. It won't start at no five to four. It won't start at no two to one. Or four to one. Or six to one. IT'S A TEN-TO-ONE WINNER I've got here. Ten-to-one winner. And what am I charging for the name of this horse? What am I charging for this ten-to-one winner. Not a pound. Not twenty bobs. Not . . .'

And so on. I have omitted much of the repetition. I stared fascinated. He utterly convinced me, this little bird-faced man, and if I could have afforded two shillings (which was what he wanted for the envelopes containing the name of the ten-to-one winner) I should certainly have patronized him. I had to walk reluctantly on and push through the crowd to the bookmakers. It was twenty-five past two and they were doing a fine trade. I stopped in front of Tommy Feldman of Brighton and inspected his board. As I looked he licked his great thumb and erased the figures '11–10' opposite Irene and wrote in '1–1' with a piece of chalk. Irene was the favourite. For the half-crown (held ready in my hot, sticky hand) I was prepared to wager I should only get, if Irene won, another half-crown. I looked at the board for the name of Murder Most Foul.

When I found it my heart gave a great leap: against it was '10–1'. Here, surely, was Billy from Newmarket's ten-to-one winner. I discarded Irene in an instant and went boldly up to Tommy Feldman. 'Half a crown to win on Murder Most Foul,' I said in a trembling voice.

Tommy Feldman took the coin nonchalantly, dropped it into a leather bag and gave me a green card with his name and a number on it. 'Twenty-five bob to half a crown Murder,' he croaked to a man who crouched at his side writing in a ledger.

I was elbowed aside by other backers, and started to dodge between people to the rails. Already, from the direction of the stand, the horses were cantering down the course towards me and the starting gate. I had always thought Stubbs idealized the racehorses he painted, but these were just like his – the small head, the snake neck, the phenomenal smoothness of the limbs at the joints, and the lovely clear shining colours (bay, brown, black) against the green grass and the blue-and-white sky. I saw Number 2, Irene, come past – a grey mare with a powerful rump – and then Murder Most Foul, chestnut, almost yellow, the jockey wearing a red and purple hooped shirt and a purple cap. My heart came into my throat as I watched it, as though it was I who was going to run.

The starting gate was away to my left and I could not see it. But soon I heard a roar from the crowd and I knew the race had begun. When I first saw the horses they were clotted together in a mass of colour on the rails, but as they flew nearer I could see that out in front of them was the grey. I feverishly looked for the red and purple hoops. The horses thudded past and disclosed poor Murder Most Foul, lolloping along last but one. They quickly disappeared towards the stand, where the winning post was, but I heard all around the fatal words, 'Irene's won it.' In a minute or two the numbers of the first three horses were hoisted up in a frame and on top was Number 2. Murder Most Foul was nowhere. I kicked myself on the ankle for being a fool and went back to the side of the beer tent to count my money.

Whichever way I counted it there was only two shillings and sevenpence. It seemed to me then that the chief regret of my life would always be that I hadn't been content to win a modest half-crown on Irene. But still, I had my return ticket to Charing Cross and two and sevenpence, and Kekewich was (I hoped) still in the stand. I turned over a page of my race card and looked at the runners for the next race. It was over a mile and six furlongs and there were fourteen runners. I studied them and then went over and looked at the odds on the bookies' boards and then studied the horses again. I tried not to give undue favour to any horses whose names suggested the case which I was investigating. On the grass I found a discarded morning newspaper, so I read the racing columns of that, too. In the end I decided on a horse called Red Harvest: its price at that time was a hundred to eight. I stood in the little queue for Tommy Feldman, in a tightly wound state of excitement.

In front of me was a short, thick man wearing a check suit and a cap. When he took off the cap to mop his perspiring head he revealed a great yellowish wen half-covered by greasy strands of grey hair. I was in the mood to observe and note every detail of the scene.

The man with the wen said: 'A fiver to win Wystan.'

A five-pound note disappeared into Tommy Feldman's satchel. My jaw dropped a little: I don't think I had realized that betting was going on other than in half-crowns and five shillings. But I was confronting Tommy Feldman and it was too late to draw back. Extremely diffidently I said, 'A shilling each way Red Harvest,' and held out a shilling, a sixpence, and six pennyworth of coppers.

Tommy Feldman was not shocked or even offensive. He said merely (the voice hoarse, the mouth with white, drying saliva at the corners): 'Buzz off, young 'un. We don't take no shilling bets.'

But if the contempt was implied it was no less profound. I slunk away, hoping no one had heard, and wishing I was at home with Mrs MacBean asking me if I fancied anything particular for supper. When I had (shiftily I am sure) looked about and made certain that the whole incident had passed without notice, I revived a little and started to wonder first, if I dare try some other bookmaker with my shilling each way, and secondly, whether I ought to back not Red Harvest but Wystan on which five good pounds of someone's money had certainly been wagered. Wystan was six to one.

I walked along the row of bookmakers, looking for the seediest. This proved to be 'Sammy Keen of New Cross. A Straight Deal.' I got in his queue. By a curious chance the man with the wen was in front of me again, still mopping his head at intervals. His presence made me acutely undecided about which horse to back. But when it was his turn he said, surprisingly, proffering his five-pound note, not Wystan but Red Harvest. It was slightly odd, but very reassuring. I held out my money and said, once again: 'A shilling each way Red Harvest.'

Sammy Keen pushed back his stained Homburg a little further. 'Come off it,' he said wearily and looked over my head for his next client.

I said in despair, 'Can I have two shillings to win Red Harvest?'

'This ain't a Sunday-school trip,' he said, as he took my money. 'Twenty bob to two Red Harvest.'

I was alarmed. 'But it's a hundred to eight, isn't it?'

He jerked his head. 'Can't you read?'

I looked at his board and there was Red Harvest, marked at 10-1. I blushed with shame and tears came into my eyes as I walked away. I felt the world to be a cruel place and its inhabitants heartless rogues.

I came up to the man with a wen, who was lighting a cigar. When it was thoroughly going he strolled over towards Joe Cape of Brixton. I followed his rather shabby figure, out of curiosity, wondering whether he was going to put more money on Red Harvest or on Wystan. When it came his turn in the queue, he said, to my surprise: 'Five pounds Libido.'

I did not know whether I was ignorant of racing ways or whether it really was extraordinary for one man to back three different horses in the same race. And then, as I watched him, I saw that he was making for another bookmaker. I pressed through the crowd after him.

This time he had five pounds to win on The Old Man, which was the favourite. I could see no system in his betting, and I kept to his heels with an intense curiosity which made me forget the rebuffs I had had. By the time the horses were coming down to the starting-gate he had backed nine of them with nine different bookmakers. And then, instead of going to the rails to watch what was happening to his money, he walked into the beer tent. That, I thought, was the way to bet – recklessly and nonchalantly.

I was too late to pick out Red Harvest going down. For this long race the horses were started farther round the course and had to take a long curve to the stand, instead of the straight stretch as in the last race. But when they passed me they were still going at a most leisurely pace and two of the jockeys were having a conversation. Red Harvest, a powerful black horse, was lying fourth or fifth and going well, I thought. It simply had to win.

*

As may be guessed, it didn't win. My experiences that day were all of a piece. The galling thing was that Red Harvest was second, and so if the wretched bookmakers had taken my shilling each way I should have saved my money and won a little besides. And in the subsequent races I might have won enough to get into the stand, track down Kekewich and solve the whole case.

After Red Harvest's race I had sevenpence left. My thirst was like the Ancient Mariner's and I blued sixpence on an extortionately expensive glass of lemonade. I watched two more races in a lacklustre way and then I went to the main gates of the racecourse and sat uncomfortably, but hidden, in a patch of nettles, hoping to see Kekewich leave early. An hour passed like a month and then gradually the whole race crowd started to come away. It would have been impossible to pick out one man, so I started the long trek down the hill to the station. I will not describe the rigours of the journey home. My detective fever had all gone and the crowd at the station and the packed trains worked on me in cold blood. Whatever, I thought, as I sat on someone's boot in the corridor, had prompted me to come on such a wild-goose chase? I could not recapture in the least my mood and theories of the morning. I conjured up the scene in court at the instant of the shot and tried to remember accurately whether it *was* the flash and the disposition of Kekewich and the murdered man or merely Kekewich's sinister personality which had made me suspicious. But, lunchless and tealess, all I could think of was food. Tomorrow, I decided, I would go to the inquest, find out from

Toller the state of the case, and then wait until the whole solution was in the newspapers. The role of private detective could, clearly, only be assumed successfully by the adult, the rich, and the lucky.

The penny I had left only took me half-way from Charing Cross to Chelsea. It was the final hideousness. I dragged my burning feet somehow along the rest of the way, crawled upstairs, and flung myself into a bath. While I lay steaming I got on the house telephone to Mrs MacBean.

'Is my father in for supper, Mrs Mac?' I asked.

She said he wasn't.

'What *is* for supper, Mrs Mac?' I said.

'A didna know ye were comin',' she said in her Glasgow tones, which I shall not go on attempting to reproduce. 'It's the cold beef again, Master Frederick.'

'Again?'

'Again,' she said.

'What about bacon and egg.'

'All right, if you prefer it.'

'I prefer it. Ten minutes?'

'Twenty minutes. The table's no' set.'

'And, Mrs Mac – two gallons of lemonade.'

'Ach,' she said and rang off.

Over that wonderful supper I read a book by H. G. Wells, called *The First Men in the Moon,* but as my mind cleared and my body revived, a desire for virtue and accomplishment overtook me and I determined to go to my room and read the book set by Mr Waggon, my dull but grotesque form-master, as a holiday task and which my father was constantly sarcastic about.

When I could eat no more Camembert I went upstairs and searched for the holiday task book. I found it at length in my suitcase under a pair of dirty white flannels with an old piece of toffee sticking to it. Melmoth, the cat, was lying on my easy-chair, in a stupor of sleep. When I touched him he made a noise like a parrot, but did not move. I poked him and he rolled coyly on his back, his fore-paws tucked in, his eyes still closed. 'Fool cat,' I said and put him down on the floor. His pretty, scarred face regarded me blearily and, I thought, reproachfully, for a moment, and then he walked off, leaving each paw momentarily behind him in turn. I sat down, removed the toffee from the book, opened it, and read:

THE BLACK DWARF
By
Sir Walter Scott, Bart.

I skipped half a dozen pages of introduction and got stuck into the first chapter. One of Scott's weaknesses is his reproduction of long conversations in dialect – his stories are peopled with verbose Mrs MacBeans. With the help of two or three breaks to get an apple and some caramels, I managed to plough through the initial *longueurs* of *The Black Dwarf.* I even got to Chapter Three, and there I started to read with an obscure but acute sense of excitement which was certainly not a result of the text alone. The story at this point tells how Earnscliff and Hobbie, on Mucklestane-Moor, see before them, in the moonlight, 'a form, apparently human, but of a size much less than ordinary, which moved slowly among the large grey stones, not like a person intending to journey onward, but with the slow, irregular, flitting movement of a being who hovers around some spot of melancholy recollection.' You see the style. Hobbie is terrified, but Earnscliff goes on, and as the figure is approached it is seen to be under four feet tall and 'its form, as far as the imperfect light afforded them the means of discerning, was very near as broad as long, or rather of a spherical shape, which could only be occasioned by some strange physical deformity'. Earnscliff hails this curious apparition and has some conversation with it – which on its side is fierce and raving – and they eventually go on their way. Earnscliff determines to visit it again the next day.

At the beginning of Chapter Four I paused a little, and looked out through the window at the deep night sky. The unusual events of the day had left me sensitive. I had a rush of intense feeling, and my scalp crawled.

In the absolute stillness of the room I bent my head and continued reading. Earnscliff and Hobbie set off for the moor again and soon come across the figure of the night before. It is engaged in piling huge stones so as to make a rough enclosure. Hobbie speaks to it. 'The being whom he addressed raised his eyes with a ghastly stare, and, getting up from his stooping posture, stood before them in all his native and hideous deformity.' And then follows Sir Walter's excellent and vivid description of – of course – the Black Dwarf. This being settles on the moor. People give him food and so on, and in return he advises them on their diseases and those of their cattle. And then I read – with no less of a horrid shock because I suspected something of the sort was coming: 'He gave these persons to understand that his name was Elshender the Recluse, but his popular epithet soon came to be Canny Elshie, or the Wise Wight of Mucklestane-Moor.' Elshie! Elshie!

A sudden gust in the night air blew the window noisily to. I started up and dashed with ridiculous alarm to the library. It was just the same as the previous night; my father was sitting there reading, and stared with disfavour on my abrupt entry. Melmoth was lying on my father's knee, his nose, the colour of coral, resting on the book. He opened his eyes, and looked at me without moving the nose; clearly he, too, was not caring for the disturbance.

'Ah,' said my father. 'And how did you find Master Reeves?'

I stared at him blankly.

'How was Ronnie Reeves?' he repeated. 'You are half asleep, Frederick; you stay up too late.'

'Oh, Ronnie,' I said, remembering my letter and the bottle-nosed usher as though they were part of a dream. '*He's* all right. Decent lunch,' I added, as my imagination got to work. 'In the afternoon Ronnie put some fishes' heads behind one of the pictures in the dining-room. He has a mania for such things.'

'So it appears,' said my father.

'Quite mad,' I said. 'And all the family, too. His sister collects extracted teeth.'

'I hope she showed you them *after* lunch.'

I sat down in an easy-chair opposite my father.

'But don't let's talk about the Reeves. How did court go?'

'Very well,' said my father, stroking Melmoth, who made, immediately, his parrot noise.

'I was sorry to miss it,' I said.

'You also missed boiled frozen mutton at the learned Registrar's.'

'Father,' I asked, 'have you read much Scott?'

'Ah,' he said, 'you are contemplating a perusal of your holiday task book.'

'I've started it. It's *The Black Dwarf* you know. Have you read it?'

'Certainly not.'

'Then you don't know what the Black Dwarf is called?'

'No. Unless he is called the Black Dwarf.'

I coughed. My father is so used to being facetious on the Bench that he cannot refrain when he is off it. 'He has other names,' I said. 'One of them is the Wise Wight of Mucklestane-Moor.'

'Indeed.'

'Another is Elshender the Recluse.'

I saw my father's eye travelling back to his book.

'And a third,' I said, very distinctly, 'is Canny Elshie.'

'Mm?'

'ELSHIE,' I said.

'Elshie,' repeated my father.

'Oh, Father,' I said, irritably, 'don't you remember? The murder yesterday. In your court. The murder of Preece. The threatening letters he was getting that Mrs Preece found were signed 'Elshie'. Didn't you listen to Inspector Toller's interview with her? The letters were signed with the name of the Black Dwarf. And – this is really the point – what sort of figure was seen running out of the court after the shot?'

'What sort of figure?' said my father. 'Was it not a hunchback?'

'Of course it was. A hunchback. A dwarf. Elshie.'

My father hooked off his glasses. 'This sounds like a penny dreadful. There must be some flaw in your logic, Frederick.'

'It's not logic, it's facts,' I said, ungrammatically but vigorously. I inched my chair cosily towards my father and then lay back for a good discussion. 'Now what does it mean? What on earth does it mean?'

My father put back his glasses. 'I haven't the faintest idea,' he said.

And before I could say another thing he was immersed in his book, surrounded by that air of oblivion which experience had taught me it was useless to try to penetrate.

3   FRIDAY, 7 *September*

I T was at this stage of the case, I think, that I felt most the need of someone with whom to discuss it. On the Friday morning I woke early. A shaft of sunlight through the mustard-coloured curtains glanced off the dark green cover of *The Black Dwarf* on my bedside table and reacted on my sensitized and confused brain. First of all I could not decide whether the name of Scott's character had *really* anything to do with the signature on the letters which Preece had been receiving. If I assumed that it had, then I could not make up my mind whether or not the letters tied up with the hunchback who had run out of court after the murder. Kekewich, anyway, faded out of the picture; it was Mrs Preece, it seemed to me then, who took on a slightly sinister aspect – so suspiciously typical and colourless, producing the mysterious letters so pat. I blushed for my ridiculous chase after Kekewich. I had wasted a whole day.

The inquest was at eleven. I told my father that I was going; he made no objection. So after breakfast, when I had got ten shillings from him, I started off for Heathstead.

The place of the inquest was a room in the mortuary. This was a building in a curving street which led to the river. At the back of it was the gasworks; opposite was a public-house. Children were playing on the chalk-marked pavement. The sirens of the ships on the river sounded very near. Some cars were drawn up nearby and among them I recognized the black, open, rather flashy M.G. which Inspector Toller used.

In the courtroom there were not many people. I arrived at the same time as the Coroner – a small man with a mottled face, steel-rimmed spectacles, and a hard voice. The jury was sworn and then went out with the Coroner to view the body. At this convenient interval I looked carefully round the court.

On the second row was Mrs Preece in another basinlike, but this time dead black, hat. In front of her sat the young solicitor who had appeared for Preece in his County Court action, Mr Sandys. Next to Mr Sandys was the shell-pink skull of Mr Brown, Savage's solicitor. It was curious to see these familiar characters in a different setting. There was no sign of Inspector Toller. The Coroner and the jury returned; the jury had the complacent and too-blasé air of those who have undergone and withstood a highly unpleasant ordeal. A moment after, Inspector Toller entered quietly but dramatically from a door at the rear of the Coroner's chair and went and stood behind the witness box. The Coroner dipped his pen in his dirty inkwell and then looked up, first at the reporters' table and then at the two solicitors on the front row.

'Who are you, please?' he said to Mr Sandys in his scraping voice.

'Sandys, sir,' said Mr Sandys, nervously half rising. 'For the widow, sir.'

The Coroner scratched a note, and then looked interrogatively at Mr Brown.

'My name is Brown, sir,' said Mr Brown. 'I appear with a watching brief for an interested party.'

The Coroner scowled, as though Mr Brown had called him a rude name, and then nodded to the policeman at his elbow.

I was astonished at the brevity of the proceedings, though perhaps I shouldn't have been. It was obvious that unless Toller had solved the case or had no immediate hope of solving it he would not let the Coroner's Court take the thing very far. Very shortly he gave evidence of being called to the Heathstead County Court on Wednesday, 5 September, and of finding the dead body of a man. Then a doctor said that he had examined the body on that occasion and had afterwards assisted in making a post-mortem, the result of which (if I understood the medical technicalities) was that he could say that the deceased had died as the result of being shot in the chest with a gun – the calibre of which I have forgotten. The Coroner treated every scientific phrase as if it were being used by the doctor in order to bamboozle the court. Finally, Mrs Preece went into the box and quietly identified the deceased as her husband, William Alfonso Preece.

I paid particular attention to Mrs Preece. There she was, a dowdy, pale, middle-aged woman of the lower middle class, but behind that appearance and place in the world – as behind the appearance and place of everyone – was somewhere the real character, the odd and distinctive individual, with a history. I was convinced that I ought to root out both character and history, for one thing because the appearance was so – in a murder case, suspiciously – typical.

As soon as she stepped down from the box the Coroner looked sourly at Inspector Toller and adjourned the inquest with the air of a man deprived by a despotic government from revealing a state scandal. I saw the Inspector about to disappear through the mysterious door at the back of the court and pressed forward to intercept him. But I was intercepted myself by Mr Sandys, who turned to me from taking leave of Mrs Preece.

'Good morning,' he said to me. 'Aren't you His Honour's son?'

I had to admit it. Out of the corner of my eye I saw Toller vanish, and I resigned myself to pumping Mr Sandys.

'Is His Honour keeping his eye on the case?' he said.

'On the contrary,' I said. 'But *I'm* interested.'

'Ah,' he said, with a hideous attempt at joviality, 'a little amateur detecting?' He was a fair-haired young man with a very healthy red face, slightly pimpled, wearing the striped tie of some sporting or old boys' organization.

'A very little,' I said, 'unless I'm too late and the case is solved?'

'Lord, no,' said Mr Sandys. 'It isn't solved yet. It's a pukka whodunnit. The police are absolutely clueless – can't even find the bloke who ran out of court when the shot was fired. Toller's been at my office two or three times. Our clerks are beginning to think *I* popped old Preece off.'

'I suppose your firm is dealing with Preece's estate.'

'Not my firm, old man,' said Mr Sandys, fingering his club tie. 'I'm only the assistant solicitor. Yes, we're handling the estate.'

'What's going to happen to the action – Preece v. Savage, the possession case?'

'Nothing,' said Mr Sandys. 'I think 2 Wren Road is far too expensive for Mrs P. to live in now her husband's dead. It's one of those awful yellow Victorian houses with a basement. It will have to be sold. We shall just withdraw the action. This is confidential, of course.'

'Mr Preece hadn't much property then?'

I think Mr Sandys saw in me a way to my father's heart and favour, because he answered remarkably freely.

'Lord, no,' he said. 'Only the house – mortgaged, of course – and a few bibs and bobs like savings certificates. But quite a big bank balance – must have won on the football pools.'

'For whom was Mr Brown appearing here today? Mr Savage?'

'Yes,' said Mr Sandys. 'Just a formality, you know. I think Savage is a bit nervous about his connexion with a murder. Which of us isn't?'

'Well, good-bye,' I said. 'Thank you for telling me so much.'

Mr Sandys said: 'Not at all. Hope to see you again when His Honour sits in Heathstead. Very sound lawyer, your father – if I may say so.' Mr Sandys went a little pink. 'Cheerio.'

When I got into the street, Toller's car had gone. The disgusting children played and screamed. The smell from the gasworks was abominable. A man leaning against the wall of the public house spat richly. I felt very disheartened. As far as I was concerned the inquest had been a complete fiasco. I wandered down the street to the main road where the trams ran and there, a few yards from the junction, I saw Toller's car parked outside a teashop.

*

Toller and Detective-Constable Jones were at a table in a corner of the tea-shop, Jones sipping coffee, Toller with a pot of tea and a plate of biscuits in front of him. I made no bones about it, but went straight up to them and said:

'Good morning. Do you mind if I join you?'

Jones looked a little surly, but Toller was very amiable.

'I saw you at the inquest,' he said, biting a biscuit with his large false teeth. 'Horrible district round here, isn't it? I always say mortuaries go along with gasworks. Not that I mind it – I was born and bred in Leeds – but young Jones here comes from leafy Bucks and takes it very badly. Are you going to have some tea, young sir?'

'Coffee, please,' I said. 'But I really came to pump you about the case.'

Toller laughed so that a little spurt of biscuit crumbs came out of his mouth. 'Fire away, then,' he said. 'But, of course, I don't promise I shall tell you anything.'

'It won't be entirely one-sided,' I said, a trifle stiffly. I could hardly bear Toller's genial condescension, but he was my only source of real news about the case and he had to be put up with. 'I have a tiny scrap of information for you.'

'Well, that's very interesting. What is it?'

'I shall leave it until you've told me all you can tell me. First of all, have you found the hunchback?'

'No,' said the Inspector, 'we haven't. That's no secret. He has absolutely disappeared. It's not to be wondered at, naturally.'

'You mean,' I said, 'that, whether he had anything to do with the murder or not, he would lie low.'

'Exactly. And if he has no police record, if we don't know his haunts, he might be able to lie low for months – years – for ever.'

'Still,' I said, 'he's a pretty conspicuous figure.'

'Maybe,' said Toller. 'But what *does* he look like? We took fifty-seven statements from the people in court and the names and addresses of thirty-odd more who hadn't seen enough to make it worth our while to take a statement. We have a description from twelve people of the man who left the court after the shot was fired. Some of those twelve say he was of normal height. Some of them say he was two feet high, some of them say he was a hunchback. Others say he was just crouching as he ran.'

'But he *was* a hunchback. I'm certain.'

'They're all certain,' said the Inspector. 'One woman is certain that he was a Negro. The point is that we haven't an accurate description and we can't arrest every man in England under four feet tall.'

'So what are you going to do about him?'

Toller took a draught of tea. 'Arthur,' he said to Jones, 'I think I'll walk back to the station. It'll do me good. You take the car and I'll join you there. You know what to carry on with.'

'O.K.,' said Jones. He nodded to me in his ungracious way and went out.

Toller leaned back in his chair and felt for his pipe. 'Conscientious young chap, that,' he said. 'Promising chap.'

'Is he?' I said, politely,

'But he gets on my nerves,' said Toller. 'Too conscientious. And too promising. He's a constable and I'm an inspector, and yet, blow me, I never feel easy with him. I sent him off so that we could have a nice confidential chat. We'll get the tram back.'

'What about the walk?'

'I never walk,' said the Inspector. 'Yes, I'd like a talk with you. Of course, I know your father well by sight. Not on this County Court Bench, but as chairman of the North Kent Quarter Sessions. Remember me to him, won't you?'

'Certainly. He knows you, too. He said you were a police officer of great experience and ability,' I said, laying it on thick.

'Did he?' said Toller, very pleased.

'He certainly did. And more besides which is too flattering to tell you.'

'You are pulling my leg, young sir,' said Toller, in great good humour.

'I'm not, honestly.'

At last we got down to the case. I think Toller was pretty truthful; that is to say, although I don't suppose he told me any confidential facts, I think he gave me an accurate indication of the line or lines the police were working on. We went on speaking, first of all, about the difficulty of tracing the hunchback.

'The point about police investigations,' Toller said – he was on his third or fourth cup of tea and was growing very expansive, 'is that where possible they proceed from the particular to the general and not vice versa. Take the hunchback. We don't go questioning every hunchback we see because we know that the hunchback we want is almost certainly not to be seen. We take the prints on the gun and see if they are in our files; if they are, perhaps we've found the hunchback at first go. In this particular case the prints aren't in our files, so we don't know whether they belong to a hunchback or not. Then we take the people who knew the deceased and see if there's a hunchback among them. In this particular case there isn't. In any event we draw up a list of people who might like to have seen the deceased deceased. And then we find out if any of those people had the opportunity to do it.'

'Who is on your list?' I asked brutally.

Toller coyly stroked his yellow chin. 'You tell me,' he said.

'Mrs Preece.'

Toller leaned towards me, so that the acrid smoke from his pipe coiled up in my face, and spoke very softly.

'Yes,' he said, 'in any murder case the surviving spouse must be the prime suspect.'

'What have you discovered about her?'

'A lot of things,' said Toller. 'She is forty-two. Preece was her second husband. She used – '

'I mean *relevant* things.'

'Who knows what things are relevant? If you mean, have we discovered that she hated her husband, that she had threatened his life, that it was her revolver, the answer is NO.'

I sighed. 'Who else is on the list?'

'Well, who?' Toller was still coy.

'I haven't the foggiest notion. *I* don't know who Preece's enemies were and whether they were in court.'

'Well, young sir, you can't expect me to tell *all* my secrets, now can you? I do like to see a young gentleman like you taking an interest in a case like this. Have you ever thought of the Force as a career? A young gentleman like you with a legal background and an education could go a long way and no mistake.'

'I'm not going to be a policeman, attractive though it is,' I said. 'I'm going to be a writer.'

'A writer!' exclaimed the Inspector, as though I had said a leper.

'Yes. As a matter of fact my first book is going to be about this case – if I can ever get to know anything about it.'

'This very case?' said the Inspector.

'Yes. Of course, I shall change the setting and alter all the names.'

'Shall I be in it?'

'You will be one of the chief characters.'

Toller had a great fit of laughing and coughing, dropped his pipe on the floor, and nearly choked. When he had recovered he said, 'Would you like to walk back to the station with me?'

'I thought you never walked.'

'I do when I have a congenial companion,' he smirked. I really do not know what Toller's attitude towards me was – whether he thought I had something useful to tell him or was one of those social, teasing characters or was humouring me because he thought my father might one day be useful to him. Anyway, we strolled together through the park.

'Has it occurred to you, Inspector,' I said, giving voice to a thought which had worried me for a long time, 'that Preece may have been shot by mistake?'

The calm sky, the still, rich trees, and the aromatic smell from a heap of burning leaves, seemed to have had a sobering effect on Toller. He replied quite seriously, fixing me with his pale blue eyes.

'What do you mean?'

'I mean that there is a curious lack of motive in the case. You don't seem to be near an arrest – and the courtroom was very crowded.'

'Yes, we've thought of that.' His voice sounded very tired, and as I glanced up at his profile I caught a new view of him; under his sallowness and flabbiness were intelligent and capable features. 'It is every policeman's nightmare – that a murderer may have killed the wrong man. The inexplicable and motiveless murder – and only to be solved by arresting and hanging an innocent man. But this is not such a case.' He walked a few more steps on his awful feet and then added: 'I hope.'

'Why not, do you think?'

'It's too fishy,' said Toller, pushing back his bowler hat.

'You mean about Elshie?'

Toller stared at me. 'What do *you* know about Elshie?'

'I was there when you saw Mrs Preece – don't you remember?'

'So you were.'

'Do you know who Elshie is?'

'No,' said the Inspector.

'I do.'

'Eh?'

'I know who Elshie is.'

The Inspector stopped and looked at me hard.

'This is the information I said I had for you,' I told him. 'And I want you to be impressed with the importance of it. I am determined to solve this case, and so I'd like as much of your cooperation as you can properly give me.'

Toller could hardly keep from laughing.

'Laugh if you want to,' I said.

'You are a card,' he said. 'How old are you?'

'Do you want to know who Elshie is?'

He said he did, and so I told him all about *The Black Dwarf*.

'So you think that the person who sent the letters to Preece and the man who was seen leaving the court after the shot were one and the same?' said Toller.

I looked at him pityingly.

'I'm inclined to agree with you,' he said, hastily. 'Don't think I'm ungrateful for this information. It is very important.'

I began to feel more satisfied.

Toller said: 'You see what education does.'

I let him talk for a while and then said, 'Now tell me what is at the bottom of this case.'

He paused to let me go out of the park gate first and dug me in the ribs as I passed. 'A card,' he said. 'This is confidential. Blackmail.'

'Of course,' I said. It seemed to me that I had really known this all the time.

'Preece was blackmailing someone. Elshie, perhaps. He put the pressure on too hard and got bumped off,' said the Inspector.

'That accounts for the comparatively large sum Preece had in the bank.'

'You'll have to become a policeman,' said Toller, admiringly. 'How *do* you get your information?'

'So the simple answer to the case,' I went on, 'is "Find Elshie".'

'Hm,' said Toller.

'Just one more question. Will you answer it truthfully? To your knowledge, has a man called Warren Kekewich anything to do with the murder?'

'No,' said the Inspector.

*

It seemed to me that in no detective story I had ever read had the amateur detective encountered such difficulties and gained less information than I had in this case. Not only that; what I knew of the case had been presented to me so ambiguously that I could get nothing clearly and logically in my mind. As I left Toller at the entrance to the local police station I determined that I would, that night, make one of those lists of possible suspects, motives, and opportunities essential to the amateur of crime. Not the least ambiguous thing about the case was Toller himself. He seemed (except in those few moments when we had talked about a possible mistake in the victim) so confident and yet, even if he had told me only a half of what the police knew, the case was as far off solution as when the globe of blood had emerged from poor Preece's mouth. Was he stupid or sly?

For lunch I went into a place not far from the police station, called the Cottage Restaurant, where, among chintz curtains and brass pots, I had toad-in-the-hole and fruit salad served by quavering genteel ladies in smocks matching the curtains. As I ate I pondered.

Clearly there was only one line of investigation possible for me to pursue, and that was Mrs Preece. She knew about Elshie's letters, and she had been in court. And also – this suddenly struck me as being very important and neglected – she knew, best of anyone, Preece; that is to say, what sort of a man he was. The bow tie, the baldish head, and the blood; that was all I knew of him and it wasn't enough. A man has to be a special sort of person to get murdered.

I pulled out the black glossy notebook which up to Wednesday I had used for poems, but which now was reserved for my notes about the case, and found (underneath this striking couplet – the beginning of a poem which I promised myself I would finish when I had found Preece's murderer and could remember what it was going to be about –

> *Dying romantically, with classic symptoms,*
> *His common family were changed to phantoms)*

the jotting I had made during Toller's interview with her of Mrs

Preece's address. I asked one of the chintzy ladies where it was and then strolled along towards it.

It was a dull and heavy afternoon. Opposite the Cottage Restaurant, in a little green plot, old men sat leaning on their sticks, spitting; a boy leaning against a bicycle watched two men leaning on spades in a hole in the road. I pushed self-righteously on to Mrs Preece's house – or, rather, the house in which she had rooms. It proved to be in a street of smallish terrace houses with tiny paved front gardens and dwarf walls surmounted by cast-iron railings. Clinging to the railings and littering the garden of Mrs Preece's house were some small children who stared at me as though I had two heads. Assuming a severe but remote expression, I went to the front door and rang the bell. I do not think I had any plan in mind; all I was going to do was to mention my father's name to Mrs Preece, exercise my young charm, and hope for her cooperation in giving me some information. It was information – any information – I needed in this case. I pressed the bell-push again. There was no response from within the house.

At length, one of the children in the garden – a little girl squatting, like an African native, over a pile of dust and a cracked cup – pulled her straw-coloured hair to one side and revealed an open-mouthed but not unintelligent physiognomy. 'There ain't no one in,' she said.

'Ain't there?' I said with useless mockery.

'Naow,' said the little girl.

'Are you Mrs Preece's little girl?'

But the head was bent again regarding the cup and the dust, and the tangled hair formed an apparently soundproof curtain.

'Where has Mrs Preece gone?' I asked.

There was again no reply. I sighed wearily, and then became aware of something at my back, moving against the leg of my flannel trousers like a cat. I turned round and saw a very small and pale boy standing there watching me and swaying gently in the manner of a drunken man. His blue overalls were so long that they doubled under his feet, giving him the long shoes of a music-hall comedian; his nose was dirtier than I had ever seen a nose.

'Hullo,' I said.

'Hullo,' he said, thickly.

'What is your name?'

'Dob Peas,' he said, which I interpreted as John Preece.

'Where's your mother?' I asked.

'Pictures,' he said.

This remark enraged the little girl. 'She ain't gone to the pictures. She's gone to the spiritualists,' she screamed. John retreated warily to the background.

'Where are the spiritualists?' I inquired of the little girl. She glared at me through the hair. I produced a threepenny piece and held it at her as one holds a bone at a dog. She snapped at it like a dog, too, and as I let her have it, she said:

'Harbinger Vale. Over Dennings'.'

I got nothing more out of her and so left her and John and the two younger and even more incoherent children with them and went back to Harbinger Vale. It was becoming more and more clear to me that the first essential for a private detective was not money so much as a motor car.

I found Dennings' – it was called Dennings' Health Food Shop, a very broken-down affair, with little basins of seeds and nuts in the window, and dusty jars of glucose and packets of carminative herbs. In one of the windows above the shop was a large card which said: BROTHERS AND SISTERS OF THE SPIRIT. TUESDAYS AND FRIDAYS AT THREE, MRS CINDER. There seemed no way to this upper room except through the shop, so I opened the door. A bell clanged and a man appeared behind the counter. He must have been the unhealthiest man ever to serve in a health food shop.

'The – er – spiritualists?' I asked.

He waved a yellow hand towards the back of the shop, where a staircase rose out of the gloom.

'Go on up. I expect they've started,' he said in a sepulchral but faint voice.

I could see that he was a weak and kind figure, so I said: 'You don't think I'm too young?'

'Not you,' he said, picking up a nut from a bowl on the counter and eating it in a tired way. 'Some of the ladies bring their children – much younger than you.'

I thanked him and started to climb the stairs. Half-way up I heard a hollow chord on a piano and then female voices raised in a hymn. On a door on the first landing was a replica of the card in the window above the shop. After some hesitation I opened this door gingerly and diffidently, and went in. The women sang:

> *'Our loved ones walk in clover,*
> *We dark vales of pain:*
> *Until we have passed over*
> *Nothing will be plain.'*

During this somewhat depressing quatrain I found an inconspicuous place at the back of the congregation, in a corner, next to an old lady with a grizzled beard. There were about twenty people in the room – all women, except one little man with a red nose and another man, enormously fat, who faced us behind a table. When the hymn was over, the fat man closed his eyes and said a prayer and then the congregation sat down. I saw a black hat on the front row and under it the nondescript features of Mrs Preece. I felt then that I was not suffering the embarrassment of my position in vain.

The room was ill-lit. A grimy crimson paper covered the walls. There was a curiously oppressive atmosphere about, and a smell of rotten apples which probably emanated from Dennings's. Behind the fat man was a sort of cubicle constructed from thin black material. He said:

'Sisters and brothers and friends. Now I have to introduce someone who needs no introduction.' He paused for effect. 'Mrs Cinder!'

With a grandiloquent gesture he pulled back the material which formed the front of the cubicle. It stuck, unimpressively, half-way, but after a little trouble he managed to reveal, sitting on a high-backed chair in the cubicle, a tiny middle-aged lady with a mass of dyed black hair who regarded us with the beady eyes of a bird. Everyone stared back in a rapt way.

'It will be the usual procedure,' went on the fat man, in a business-like manner. 'Absolute silence until, through Mrs Cinder, the Control addresses us, and then questions and answers, please, only from those sisters, brothers, and friends with whom, the control is communicating. And let us hope and pray for guidance and good cheer from our loved ones who have passed over – and for a well-disposed Control. I mean not Spotty.'

This last phrase was evidently some well-established private joke among the brothers and sisters, for, in spite of the solemnity of the occasion, it was greeted by a little titter. The fat man walked to the back of the room and drew a curtain across the window. The room was then in darkness save for a faint violet light from a lamp on the ceiling directed on Mrs Cinder. The bird-eyes glittered for a few moments and then closed; the fat man returned to the cubicle and drew the material across, making Mrs Cinder invisible. The violet light glowed on the black cloth.

Except for the bearded woman next to me who kept taking pieces of bread out of her hand-bag and champing them with a collapsing mouth, there was utter quiet, and although I knew that the whole thing was complete nonsense, I could not help feeling an anticipatory warmth at the pit of my stomach. The quiet must have lasted at least five minutes; my anticipation changed, after about two, to boredom. I wondered whether I could decently creep out and wait for Mrs Preece in the unsmelly air of the street.

And then, sending a cold trickle down my back and prickling my scalp, there came from within the cubicle a number of low but agonizing groans. The front cloth of the cubicle was agitated, as though behind it someone was struggling with a deadly enemy. The groans became louder and more frequent. Mrs Cinder, clearly, was going into a trance.

Eventually the noises and the disturbance died down, and out of the quietness and from within the cubicle came a deep male voice, speaking precisely but with a foreign accent.

'Hullo, everybody, please,' said the voice.

The fat man said: 'Is that Ram Verjee?'

'Here is Ram Verjee,' said the voice.

The fat man pulled back the curtain again and the edge of the spot-light caught a vague face surmounted by a sort of turban, the whole suspended in the air, like the face of the Cheshire Cat, at the top of the cubicle. This apparition was visible only for a moment or two and was then whisked away, allowing the spot-light to fall once more on the countenance of Mrs Cinder. The beady eyes were now closed, the countenance was deathly pale, drops of sweat glistened on the forehead.

'Did you glimpse me, please?' said the foreign voice.

'Yes, Ram Verjee,' replied the fat man, 'you were visible to all.'

'It is difficult for us here,' said Ram Verjee, 'to make ourselves – .' Here, the voice broke off and resumed, a second later, in muffled and angry tones. 'Go away, little girl,' said Ram Verjee, 'and be careful, please, with that tennis racquet.'

'Ram Verjee,' said the fat man, 'there are many of us here today waiting for news of those who have passed over. Have you anything to tell us?'

Ram Verjee had recovered his bland air. 'It is difficult for us to wrap around ourselves enough of the earth-stuff to make us seeable by your eyes. I wish that I could make all here visible to you. In the beautiful light of the sun, along emerald avenues of foliage, walk the shining spirits of this eternal world. From I know not where comes a swelling music which tells of cares lost for ever, happiness always, and of peace always. Peace – that is the characteristic of our life now. The peace that passeth – Little girl, if you don't go away I shall be very angry indeed. And mind what you are doing with that tennis racquet. Careful now, careful. Ow!' Ram Verjee uttered a cry of pain.

There was a pregnant pause. Mrs Cinder stirred uneasily in her trance. And then from the air in front of her came a female child's asinine giggle.

'Spotty here. Spotty here,' said a babyish voice. 'Hello! Spotty's got a new tennis racquet. A real dinky one. Wish you could all see it. S'got green on it and white and a *real* rubber handle. S'called the Bijou Champion Tennis Racquet and Spotty's Uncle George gave it Spotty.'

'Spotty,' said the fat man, pleadingly. 'What has happened to Ram Verjee?'

'Spotty hit Ram Verjee with Spotty's Bijou Champion Tennis Racquet.'

There was a good deal of this sort of disembodied horseplay which I found very tedious. But at length the spiritual control known as Ram Verjee got total possession of Mrs Cinder's body and the frightful Spotty became silent. The fat man and Ram Verjee had a short sententious conversation and then Ram Verjee said something which made me sit up in my chair and crane forward to catch every word.

'Our two worlds have recently suffered a disturbance,' said Ram Verjee. 'When the passing-over of a man is sudden and violent there is as much agitation in this existence as in yours. That happened a little while ago. In your world a shot; in ours a man unprepared for the life we lead here. Ah, what a life it is! I see them now, walking through the bright trees, glowing like the minarets on the Taj Mahal – beautiful, immortal, happy beings...'

He went on and on, and I sat back again. As he spoke, a ghostly tambourine drifted through the violet spot-light and gave a few desultory rattles. It was all the most obvious and boring fraud. I wondered whether the reference to Preece would be pursued. It was.

The fat man said: 'Is he there – the man who passed over violently?'

'There is someone here,' said Verjee. 'He is asking for Matilda.'

'Is it him?' said the fat man.

'No, no,' said Ram Verjee. 'Is Matilda there?'

A voice came from the audience – it might have been Mrs Preece's, but I wasn't sure. 'Tell him that Matilda's here.'

'Matilda's here,' said the fat man. 'What is the message?'

Ram Verjee said: 'A message for Matilda. Tex says not to worry.'

'What is that name?' asked the fat man.

'Tex,' said Ram Verjee. 'T-E-X.'

The voice from the audience called again. 'How do I know it is really Tex?'

Ram Verjee said: 'Tex says, "Could you still shoot the cigar out of my mouth, Matilda?"'

There was a single female gasp from the audience. 'Is that right?' said the fat man. After a little pause, the voice from the audience said faintly, 'Yes.'

And then the hideous child-impersonator voice came back. 'Yoo-hoo! Yoo-hoo! Spotty here again.'

So it went on for nearly an hour. Spotty was got rid of, Ram returned, a trumpet floated in the violet light. Grandmothers, uncles, old sweethearts, and the Duke of Wellington sent messages, usually through Ram, but sometimes in person. At one point a long stream of what looked like cotton wool came out of Mrs Cinder's mouth; the fat man said it was ectoplasm. Spotty recited 'Christopher Robin is saying his prayers'. At last Mrs Cinder started groaning and shifting about in her chair; the fat man said that she was coming out of the trance, and drew the curtain of the cubicle.

He drew the curtain back from the window, too, and everyone blinked and looked round sheepishly but defiantly as when the lights go on in a cinema after a film at which people have been weeping. Mrs Preece was still on the front row. As we stood up to sing a hymn the bearded woman next to me swallowed a piece of bread and said fervently:

'Beautiful, wasn't it?'

*

Before it was all over there was a silver collection. When the box came to me I saw some ten-shilling notes in it. Mrs Cinder evidently had as tight a half-Nelson over these poor women as horse-racing had over their husbands. When we all left I kept at a handy but discreet distance behind Mrs Preece. She had not seen me. In the street, I was relieved to see that she set off on her bow legs, walking alone. I waited until we were crossing the heath, and then caught her up.

'Good afternoon, Mrs Preece,' I said, cheerily.

She turned round and showed a rather startled face. 'Yes,' she said. 'What is it?'

'Perhaps you don't remember me. I was with Inspector Toller at the court last Wednesday. My name is French. I am Judge French's son.'

I hoped deceitfully to convey to her that my connexion with the case was on some sort of official basis, but she looked dubious.

'Oh,' she said.

I laid on some more deceit. 'With Inspector Toller's approval I've been pursuing independent investigations and I thought perhaps I might have a little talk with you.'

She was wary. 'Mr Sandys is looking after my affairs.'

'Oh yes,' I said, easily. 'I had a chat with Mr Sandys after the inquest this morning.'

She wavered and I stood firm.

'What was it you wanted to ask me about?' she said.

I took her arm in its dingy black dress and urged her gently towards an empty bench. 'Shall we sit down for a few moments,' I said soothingly.

When we were seated she looked at me from under the brim of her unlovely hat. 'You are a strange boy and no mistake,' she remarked.

I coughed and looked severe and got the conversation back on an impersonal level. 'I wanted to ask you,' I said, 'whether you have found out who Elshie was. I thought that perhaps looking through Mr Preece's papers might have given you some more information.'

She shook her hat. 'I told the Inspector all I know.' She smoothed the handbag she was carrying as though it were made of delicious fur. 'He keeps coming to see me, you know,' she added.

'Why?' I said, brutally.

She turned and burst out in what was for her a very lively way: 'What do you think?'

'You can guess what I think.' I was determined to let her show me something of what lay beneath that almost caricature-like appearance of hers.

'You're just like everyone else.' She was really moved. 'I don't know anything about it. Bill's death – what happened – I don't know anything about it. It's all strange to me. It happened to him in another world he was living in, what I knew nothing about.' She turned her face away again. 'He was a quiet sort of chap.'

I let her look over the cropped grass of the heath towards the far, stuccoed, cubed Victorian houses, very clear in the still, late-afternoon air, and then loaded and discharged my howitzer.

'Who is Tex?' I said.

It landed plumb on the target. She positively jumped. 'How do you know – ? You were at the spiritualists.'

'I was at the spiritualists.'

Her whole manner was changed – livelier, younger, less stupid. 'Does *he* know?' she said.

'Who?'

'The Inspector.'

'What about?'

'Tex.'

'Why should he know?'

'He might have traced it all back.'

I felt myself growing somewhat bemused, but I struggled to retain my air of omniscience. 'Could he do that?' I asked her.

'I don't know. I don't know,' she wailed, in a womanly way. And then she said sharply, 'And now you'll tell him, anyway.'

I leapt at this bargaining lever. 'Not necessarily. Officially, of course, I have nothing to do with the police. I tell them just as much or as little as I like. All I'm interested in is solving the case.'

'Tex has nothing to do with the case,' she said.

'How do I know?'

'You'll have to take my word for it,' she said, stiffening her resistance.

'The Inspector might not take it.'

'You see,' she cried, 'you *will* tell him! Look here, how much do you know about Tex?'

'As much as Ram Verjee,' I said. 'But I want to know a good deal more. Someone killed Mr Preece by shooting him very accurately, very accurately indeed. Someone, perhaps, who was accustomed to shooting cigars out of Tex's mouth.'

'You little beggar,' she whispered, clutching my wrist with a surprisingly lobster-like grip.

'Come on, Mrs Preece,' I said, concealing my nervousness. 'You might as well tell me the whole story. What have you to fear if you didn't kill Mr Preece?'

'I'll tell you what I've got to fear.' She leaned back on the bench and put her chin in her hand. 'I was born in a caravan,' she said, after a pause. 'My mum and dad used to travel about with fairs. They had a show – a giant rat it was at one time. Then a live, six-legged pig. And then the mermaid from the Andaman Islands – she was stuffed. And the living Torso. And Thomasina Thumb. Show people we were. That's how I met Tex.'

To my embarrassment she suddenly took off her hat. 'Once upon a time,' she said, 'I was quite a good-looking girl. Look at my hair – it's still nice, isn't it?' It was certainly luxuriant and a rich auburn, arranged in a sloppy bun. 'Tex did a Wild-West turn – stock whip, lariat – you know the thing. We met up with him at Darlington. We were married at Newcastle and I left Mum and Dad's show and went with Tex. He blossomed out then. Bought a horse. I was dressed as a cow-girl.'

I looked at her in amazement. Cow-girl, indeed!

'Tex taught me how to shoot,' went on Mrs Preece. 'With a pistol. In the end we had a very good show and we went into a circus. One of the things we did was Tex would be smoking a cigar and I would shoot it out of his mouth. It wasn't really as dangerous as it sounds. The cigar used to be in a long holder and Tex wasn't far away. But the act went down very well.'

Was this all true! I gazed at Matilda Preece, plumbing her to the depths; the astonishing hair glinted in the level rays of the sun.

'It didn't last,' she said. 'One day in Birmingham Tex left me. He ran away with another girl and I never saw him again. Not from that day to this.'

'But,' I said, 'isn't he ... passed over? This afternoon Ram Verjee said that – '

'I don't know,' cried Mrs Preece. 'That's just it. I don't know. I hope so.'

'You hope Tex is dead?'

'Of course I do. Don't you see? I married Bill Preece without knowing whether Tex was dead, without getting a divorce. I'm a bigamist, that's what I am. A bigamist. Now tell the Inspector – I don't care. It's haunted me for sixteen years, haunted and worried me. I'll be glad to get it over and get to prison.'

I sat petrified with unease; now I had unearthed the skeleton I would have given anything to bury it again.

'Oh,' I said, in a small voice. 'But, Mrs Preece, surely they wouldn't prosecute you for bigamy after all those years – sixteen years?'

'They never forget – the police,' she said, bitterly. 'And once they get poking about into the past and discover Tex, they'll have me, you'll see.'

'I shan't tell them about the bigamy, of course,' I said. 'It can't have anything to do with the case. But what about your being a crack shot?'

'I don't know as I am a crack shot. I haven't handled a gun since Tex left me. I never had the heart to do it. I went straight back to Mum and Dad. They'd given up the show by then. They had a second-hand shop at Wembley. Nobody knew me. When Bill Preece asked me to marry him I married him.'

My detective faculties were paralysed; here was Mrs Preece, except for Elshie, the most important personage in the case, unburdening her very soul, and I could think of nothing pertinent to ask her.

'And when did you come to Heathstead?' I asked, aimlessly.

'Twelve years ago. Bill's Aunt Lily left him 2 Wren Road in her will. I never liked it. Too big. Great big dark house it is – great big rooms, great big cellars. Big enough for a factory. I was glad when we had to leave it. I didn't want to go back to it, but the digs are so dear. Well, that's what started it all, isn't it?'

'Yes,' I said. I was completely fogged. And when she stood up to go I could offer no objection.

'I don't care whether you tell the Inspector or not,' she said. She put her hat on and became again the tired, anonymous housewife.

'I appreciate your giving me your confidence,' I said. 'You can rest assured that I shan't abuse it.'

'You're a queer boy,' she said. We gazed at each other for long seconds, trying to fathom each other's mind. And then she started to stump off over the grass. I watched her bow-legged figure until it was lost among the traffic which ran along the perimeter of the heath. Spotty, Ram Verjee, and Thomasina Thumb whirled in my brain. Wasn't it, after all, a simple case? Had Matilda Preece shot, as easily as the cigar out of Tex's, that bubble of blood out of her husband's mouth?

*

I went straight back to Chelsea. After my extraordinary day the house seemed strange yet familiar, and very comforting. Mrs

MacBean said that my father was in for dinner, so I changed into a dark suit. I found him in the sitting-room drinking sherry.

'I have just had a severe shock, Frederick,' he remarked. 'MacBean tells me there are only six and a quarter dozen of this sherry left. That will scarcely see my time out. As for you, poor boy, when your sherry days arrive you will probably have to drink *Empiroso*. What dreadful mornings you will have!'

'I shall know no better.'

'Very true.'

'But perhaps I had better have a small glass of this before the rats get at it.'

My father sighed and poured me one. I reclined on the settee and sipped it. My father rested his elbow on the marble of the mantelpiece and looked at me keenly.

'Are you still messing about with this ridiculous case?' he said.

'Yes.'

'I shall have a policeman for a son, I can see. Well, it is the revolution of our time. Your grandfather, who, as you know, was a most distinguished Chancery silk, must have revolved in his grave when I accepted my appointment to the County Court Bench. But you, you will spend your life in a worse place – a police court. A melancholy end to a notable legal family.'

'I don't think I have enough intelligence to be a policeman,' I said. 'I am no forrader with this case.'

'You do not surprise me,' said my father.

'I should be, you know,' I said warmly. 'In a way, this is an ideal case for a private detective. There are few obvious clues, no professional criminals involved, an intellectual or literary element, and the police are baffled – I hope.'

'My dear Frederick, what urges you to waste your vacation in this slightly grotesque way? What, as I believe the Americans say, is in it for you?'

I sipped luxuriously. 'Well, on the highest level I think that the hunt for a murderer – fictional or in real life – satisfies a moral longing. It is all a part of the revolution of our time. We – my generation – have no general and dogmatic views about right and wrong. And yet we want good to be rewarded and evil punished. Murder is a happening which usually is quite unarguably evil even from our disillusioned viewpoint. And so in that little limited sphere we have a disproportionate interest. On a lower level, of course, the pursuit of a murderer has the interest of a puzzle. But if you go on to ask me why men are fascinated by puzzles, I am afraid I cannot answer you.'

'I begin to think, Frederick,' said my father, pouring himself, rather hurriedly, another glass of sherry, 'that the school I chose for you is somewhat too advanced. Perhaps you should have gone to Wellington.'

'Father, do you think you can be serious for a few minutes and give me your advice?'

'I have never been serious since I was commissioned as an infantry officer in the 1914-18 war.'

'You remember, no doubt,' I went on remorselessly, 'that a man named William Alfonso Preece was murdered in your court last Wednesday.'

'Vividly,' said my father.

'Today I attended the inquest. It was adjourned – nothing came out of it. The hunchback, Elshie, the man who left the court after the shot, has not been found yet. I have discovered that the wife, Mrs Preece, is a dab shot with a pistol – but she has no more the psychology of a murderer than – than Mrs MacBean.'

'Mrs MacBean is about to murder us both – with a garlicy goulash.'

'I had a hunch about a sinister solicitor who was in court at the time of the murder, but when I investigated him I found his office and his life perfectly normal. Now where do I go from here? What possible line of investigation is there for me?'

'Savage,' said my father.

'What?'

'The name of the defendant in the case was Savage, wasn't it? I should have thought, my dear Sherlock, that where a plaintiff was murdered in court – and especially a plaintiff who was going to be successful – the obvious and immediate suspect would be the defendant.'

'But, Father, you were there afterwards when Savage's solicitor – a man absolutely above suspicion – came forward and said that Savage couldn't possibly have fired the shot.'

'To that,' said my father, 'I have two replies. First, no man in any criminal case is above suspicion – and this man especially. The solicitor to an unsuccessful defendant! Come, Frederick, you are losing your grip.'

'Be serious, Father.'

'And secondly,' continued my father, 'supposing the solicitor to be above suspicion – which I do not admit – and that Savage could not have fired the shot, do you suppose that it is impossible for Savage to have hired, or arranged for, or persuaded, a third party actually to do his dirty work for him? Motive, Frederick, motive is what one must look for, and if you are satisfied that Preece's wife did not kill him, then you must turn to someone else with a grudge – his opponent in litigation, the man he was trying to drag from hearth and home, the tenant of (was it not?) 2 Wren Road. In a word, Savage.'

This was all, I knew, an elaborate leg-pull on my father's part, but it burst on me with revelatory force. I wanted more than anything to discuss, or at least to ponder, the ideas which my father's remarks had caused to flood my mind, but at that instant the puce face of my father's dinner guest, Admiral Crowborough-Crow, appeared round the sitting-room door. He was a neighbour of ours, recently retired and writing his memoirs. The conversation turned to vintage port in which he and my father had a mutual interest. Shortly afterwards the dinner bell went and we all took our digestions downstairs to deal with Mrs MacBean's goulash.

*

After dinner my father and the Admiral played chess. I escaped to my room. It had taken on permanently, it seemed to me, the highly charged atmosphere of these last few nights. The open window, the foliage in the square, the moths, the lamplight, and, on my bedside table, the green volume of *The Black Dwarf,* all seemed to have a strange and disturbing significance. From somewhere in the square came the human, emotional voice, which Melmoth used only to other cats. Into its late-Wagnerian harmonies another and coarser voice suddenly broke which could only belong to a rather ridiculous cat which lived nearby and wore a collar with its name – MACK – on it. I sharpened a pencil out of the window and then sat at the table with my notebook in front of me. 'LIST OF SUSPECTS,' I wrote at the head of a blank page, and then, slowly and with a good deal of thought, the following:

Name	*Remarks*	*Next move*
1. MATILDA PREECE	If so, why did she do it in court? Did Preece know about Tex?	Find out how she got on with Preece.
2. WARREN KEKEWICH	But what motive?	Follow him again.
3. SANDYS	A ridiculous suspect.	Only when all else fails.
4. ELSHIE	Must this necessarily be the hunchback? Has the h–b *really* anything to do with it?	No next move, alas! Wait till Toller finds him – and then the case will be over, perhaps!
5. SAVAGE	No opportunity. Motive – lunatic resentment at Preece winning the case? Must never forget that Preece was killed in court, at almost the precise moment of his victory. This certainly points to Savage – or to Savage's accomplice. Has Savage a wife? He has certainly a solicitor.	Go to Heathstead and investigate Savage.
6. BROWN	Suppose Brown was lying when he said Savage did not fire the shot. Under what circumstances could an ex-Mayor of Heathstead protect the defendant in a little possession case?	Go to Heathstead and investigate Brown – when Sandys fails.
7. TEX	If he is still alive! Since Ram Verjee (i.e. Mrs Cinder) knew something about Tex, Mrs Preece's past must be gossiped about in Heathstead.	Find out who told Mrs. Cinder
8. X	This is the man Savage hired, arranged for or persuaded to bump off Preece.	*Quién sabe?*

What a nebulous lot of suspects, I thought, when I had finished this table. If only I could find Elshie or break Savage's alibi! And very probably the murderer was not on the list at all. I realized that my investigations – including my long talk with Mrs Preece – had told me nothing about Preece. What was it she had said about him? – he was 'a quiet sort of a chap'. That was of no importance. But it irritated a remote part of my mind that she *had* said something important, if I could only get the conversation in a proper perspective. I had the feeling that I had so far been looking at the case with the telescope wrong way round. I leaned out of the window into the warm night.

Below, on the front steps, the Admiral was taking leave of my father. The air was so still that the aroma of their cigars floated up to me. The Admiral's foreshortened figure, shaped like a dinghy, rowed itself off, and my father looked up and saw me.

'What are you doing?' he called.

'Making a list of suspects. Shall I add you?'

My father tore his imaginary hair. 'Go to bed. Go to bed.'

4 SATURDAY, 8 *September*

IT bores me to write it – it must be even more boring to read it – but I went to Heathstead the next morning after breakfast. My life was assuming the repetitive pattern of a compulsive neurotic's. I was armed with my notebook and three pounds drawn from my post-office savings account. Heathstead was becoming dreadfully familiar; the features of the porter at the station, the somewhat similar features of the horse which always stood, attached to an ancient cab, in the courtyard – these had the symbolic quality of known but anonymous faces in dreams. In the street which led from the station to the heath the sun came brilliantly off apples in the greengrocers', the rivulet which ran from the fishmongers' across the pavements, and the backs of dogs being taken shopping by housewives. I asked a policeman where Wren Road was.

I was determined thoroughly to investigate Savage; over night my father's words had become more and more plausible. If a plaintiff is killed, investigate the defendant; it was elementary. The small voice inside which whispered, 'What do you mean – *investigate?*' I ignored. I had not the least idea how I was to approach Savage.

I walked along the edge of the heath, past an unruffled pond in which the reflection of willows looked more real than the originals, past a terrace of barrel-chested Regency houses, a girl with rabbit teeth, in jodhpurs, and then, as directed by the policeman, down a curving tree-lined street which led into Wren Road.

Wren Road must have been built about 1870; trees could not wholly smother the horror of those houses, each like a small nonconformist chapel, which lined it. The front garden of Number 2 was a jungle of rhododendron bushes, holly, and monkey-puzzle trees; those windows which could be seen were grimy; the gate had on it an old plate which read: NO HAWKERS, CIRCULARS, OR CLERGY. It said nothing about private detectives. I pushed open the gate and went up the weed-sprouting path. Standing under the iron and glass porch – a miniature Crystal Palace – I tried to find something which would waken this house of the dead. The old-fashioned bell-push was clearly not working, the knocker was so stiff it could only be raised an inch; I had to hammer on the door with my fist. I hammered and hammered. There was no answer.

In a way I was relieved; I did not relish interrogating Savage. But I intended to go back at lunch-time when someone, if not Savage, would surely be at home. In the meantime I set off for Mr Brown's office.

Can I bear to relate the details of yet another fruitless interview? It must be done, alas! I went boldly into the general office of Mr Brown's firm – which was called, impressively, Widgery, Brown, and Partridge-Fairley – and asked for Mr Brown. Copies lay about of the *Geographical Magazine* and the *Illustrated London News;* on the wall were old prints of Heathstead; the mahogany counter gleamed as discreetly as the fingernails of the girl-receptionist who entered my name in a half-calf appointments book. A greater contrast than this office and Warren Kekewich's could not be imagined. Within three minutes I was shown in to Mr Brown.

As he unfolded his length to greet me I noticed that bald head was no paler. 'I remember you, of course, Mr French,' he lisped, and then asked the receptionist to bring another cup of coffee.

So as we talked we sipped and ate Abernethy biscuits from a tin which Mr Brown extracted from a charming corner cupboard.

'You will often find crumbs in the folds of legal documents,' he remarked. 'Lawyers cannot do without their elevenses.'

I had to tell him about my interest in the murder, and apologize for taking up his time. He was extremely nice about it.

'I can't help you, I fear,' he said. 'I think you were there when I made my first statement to the police – the Scotland Yard man has been here since, of course, and he now has fuller particulars. But nothing more that materially helps the investigation.'

'It would be most discourteous of me,' I said, 'if I sat here eating your excellent biscuits and suggested that your client Mr Savage might be – involved, but – '

He laughed and smoothed down his fringe of white hair. 'Not at all. Mr Savage has been a client of the firm's for some years, and while, naturally, I cannot speak as to the entirety of his private life, so far as I know he is a quiet, respectable, and normal citizen. He is, I certainly know, very highly thought of by his employers, the Planet Engraving Company, a well-known firm in the City. Fenchurch Street, I believe, if you want to make inquiries.' I think he was pulling my leg. 'As for the actual shooting,' he continued, 'I can only say again – and my clerk, Mr Prideaux, will corroborate what I say – that it was physically impossible for Mr Savage to have done it.'

I suppose I must have looked baffled, because he laughed again and went on: 'It won't have escaped you that a conspiracy between Mr Savage, Mr Prideaux, and myself might well exist, whereby one of us committed the murder and we provided mutual alibis.'

I looked at him and involuntarily nodded.

His amusement was very great. 'I think you ought to have a word with Mr Prideaux. You can then see what a desperate character he is.'

'Although Mr Prideaux was in court with me last Wednesday,'

said Mr Brown as we walked up the stairs, 'he is not really a litigation clerk. Holidays, you know, disorganize the office at this time of year. Nor am I myself on the common law side now – young Partridge-Fairley relieved me of it many years ago. But he is on holiday, too. I never liked it. One has to have a flair for it. Do you intend to follow your father and read for the Bar?'

And so it went on until we reached the door of a room on the second floor, which Mr Brown threw open to disclose, behind a desk piled high with papers, the bald, domed head of a man aged about sixty.

'Mr Prideaux,' said Mr Brown, 'I want you to meet Mr French. Mr French is His Honour's son.'

The head rose about a foot in the air as its owner stood up. 'Very pleased to meet you, sir,' said Mr Prideaux, bowing slightly and then trotting round his desk towards us like some sort of mechanical toy. He had no legs to speak of, but he had a wonderful height of brow and a voice which contrived to be both nervous and deep. He wore black alpaca false sleeves from elbow to wrist and a collar which held his head like an egg-cup.

'Mr French is engaged in the Preece case,' said Mr Brown.

'Oh yes, sir,' said Mr Prideaux, scratching delicately at the corner of his demure mouth which was surmounted by a heavy grey moustache.

'But I think I'm going to resign from it,' I said.

Mr Prideaux joined discreetly in Mr Brown's laughter, though he had no idea he was the cause of it.

Mr Brown said: 'Mr Prideaux has been with us forty-five years.'

Mr Prideaux blushed darkly. 'It hardly seems so long as that, sir,' he said.

When we were going I heard Mr Prideaux say to Mr Brown: 'Might I have a word with you this morning? The Lawrence probate papers and the Savage conveyance, sir.'

'Come down now, if you like, Mr Prideaux,' said Mr Brown.

So we had the pleasure of Mr Prideaux's company all the way down to the ground floor. He opened all the doors for us in the manner of a first-rate butler, and managed to get in a few well-chosen words with me about the weather. I said good day to my suspects and then wandered out into the sunshine. Either I could reduce my black list by two names or Mr Prideaux and Mr Brown were the two most consummate criminals in Europe.

*

As I walked along I played with the idea of calling at Dennings' to see Mrs Cinder. But the thought of those black, mouse-like eyes and the overpowering unction of the fat man and the smell of the health food shop depressed me. I turned in at the Cottage Restaurant for an early lunch – savoury mince and baked apple. One of the chintz-garbed ladies became motherly and I resolved never to go there again.

Wren Road was still quiet when I walked down it again after lunch, and Number 2 still had its disused, impenetrable look. I knocked once more on the front door. And then I got mad and kicked it, but without any better result. A path overgrown with the long clinging tentacles of rambler roses led from the front garden to a side gate. The gate was locked, so I beat on it, and then, after a decent interval, put my shoe on the rusty latch and hoisted myself up so that I could peer through a two-inch gap between the top of the gate and a broken-down trellis over it. The passage along the side of the house to the back garden was dark, and beyond it I had a glimpse of waist-high grass and sombre evergreens. All was deserted.

I managed to get my knee in a gap in the trellis, pulled my other leg up and made the gap bigger with it, and then, smashing away like a rhino in a bamboo feast, turned round to let myself down on the other side of the gate. I brushed the cobwebs off my clothes, sucked the blood off my hands, and went cautiously along the passage.

It had a chill and sinister air, though it was only the shade of the house which made it cool and there was nothing sinister to see. But I had a feeling about it – so much so that half-way along I turned back and unbolted the side gate so that I should have an easy means of escape. What or whom did I expect to encounter? I started walking quietly again along the passage.

And then, as I walked, I knew that someone was watching me.

It is a feeling one often reads about and rarely experiences, but it is a real one and highly unpleasant, like the terror of the dark one has as a child. I went a few uneasy steps with bogus nonchalance and then wheeled round suddenly, the blood pounding in my ears.

Leaning against the post of the side gate was a girl with a cigarette between her lips. I almost laughed with relief.

'What the hell are you doing?' she asked, without removing the cigarette.

And then, succeeding the frightened feeling, came an emotion almost as bad – a horrible embarrassment as I realized that I had broken down some innocent person's trellis work and trespassed into their back garden. I went, sheepishly I believe, up to the girl.

'I'm most frightfully sorry,' I said.

'Yes,' she said, 'but what about?'

Her eyes regarded me very coolly indeed. How could I ever explain all that had led up to this?

'It sounds very foolish,' I said, 'but I was throwing a ball about in the street and it came over into your back garden. I threw it too far.'

'You certainly did,' she said.

'I knocked on the front door,' I went on, 'but no one seemed to be in, so I'm afraid I climbed over the side-gate. I'm afraid, too, that I damaged the trellis a bit more.'

Her eyes never left mine. They were a very deep but clear blue, like that of some mineral. After a silence, that for me grew every second more awkward, she said:

'I don't believe you.'

Then she gave a great suck at her cigarette and waited for me to answer. I looked her up and down. She was not so tall as I, and thin. She wore a blue frock with short sleeves. Her hair was dark brown and piled rather untidily on the top of her head, revealing her ears which were small and pointed. On the angle of her jaw bones a glistening of down showed in the rays which filtered down through the rambler roses. Her arms were hairy, too.

'Who are you?' I asked.

'Who are *you*?' she said, with more pertinence.

I told her my name and who I was. She asked me if I lived in

Heathstead, and I had to tell her I didn't. All the time we were talking I tried to weigh up the pros and cons of telling her the whole business, but I couldn't think clearly. The thing – the only thing – that was obvious to me was that she was clearly something to do with the house and, therefore, with Savage.

'Let's go on the heath,' she said, throwing away her cigarette-end, 'where we can talk freely.'

'I don't know whether I want to talk freely,' I said.

'I could give you in charge. In fact I've a good mind to give you in charge.'

I imagined myself sitting in Heathstead police station and it coming to the ears of Inspector Toller.

'What do you want to talk about?' I asked.

'Come along and see.'

Not a word passed between us until we were well on to the heath. During the walk I kept snatching little glances at her. Her features were regular, but small. Her lashes were so thick that they made her eyes look darker than they really were. Her sharp ears and her hirsuteness gave me the odd impression that she had been constructed from some animal – a little, furry one – like a denizen of Dr Moreau's island in the H. G. Wells story. We sat on the grass, not far from the bench where I had interviewed Mrs Preece.

'Now,' said the lemur-girl.

'Not so fast,' I said. 'I think I ought to know to whom I am going to unburden the story of my life.'

'You are a somewhat facetious boy,' she said, gravely. 'My name is Rhoda Savage.'

'Savage's daughter,' I said involuntarily, with a sudden memory of hearing in court about Savage's family.

'My father, not unnaturally, is called Savage,' she said. 'Mr Savage. You know him, then?'

'Not exactly. I know *of* him. You see –'

'Don't you think you had better begin at the beginning?'

I looked at her keenly. She sat with her shoulders hunched, her face expressionless. 'Very well,' I said. And I told her how I had been present at Preece's death, how I had always longed to solve the horrible but fascinating puzzle of a murder case; of my researches into Kekewich, Mrs Preece, and Mr Brown; and finally – but I stopped rather abruptly.

'And now,' she said, 'you are proposing to investigate my father.' Her rather blank look had not altered throughout my recital, and it did not change now.

'Well,' I plucked a few blades of grass. 'What do you think?'

'You don't know very much about the case, do you?' she said.

'No. But does anyone?' Something – a kind of caution – had prevented me from telling her what I knew about Elshie, but I almost blurted it out at this moment. She was, with her contained, cool, and masterful air, so maddening. 'What do *you* know about it?' I went on, remaining content for her to think me a nit-wit.

'Nothing.'

'But your father must have discussed it with you.'

'No.'

'Did your father know Preece?'

'Of course he *knew* him. You can't rent a house from a man without getting to know him. But we knew him no more than was necessary or proper.'

'What sort of man was he?'

She did not seem to have heard me. Her face was turned to the sun, she appeared to be gazing far off where from behind the white stucco of the houses fringing the heath still whiter clouds rose like Oriental architecture; as I looked at her, her mineral-bright eyes glittered with moisture. I was suddenly alarmed.

'Miss Savage. What's the matter?' My voice sounded very stupid.

She inclined her little animal face to me, and then rested her thin brown hand on my knee. Until that moment I had not thought of her as a girl at all. She seemed in a few seconds to have changed her whole character; to have become younger and less hard.

I said: 'Do tell me what's the matter.'

She took her hand away and said: 'There's nothing the matter.'

'I think there is.'

'How can I tell you?' she said in a choked and violent voice. 'You are a stranger and only a boy.'

'I don't feel that we're strangers.' (She had me talking that way, too.) 'As for my lack of age, surely you've judged by now what – what sort of boy I am.' I felt that I was on the edge of a tremendous revelation.

She gave me the kind of look that my father reserves for untruthful witnesses and kept it on me for a long half-minute.

'It was fated,' she said, 'that I should find you!'

I was half embarrassed, half excited. 'If you want me to help you, I will,' I said.

'Wait until you hear what you might have to do.'

'I don't care what it is.' Someone not myself was saying these reckless and ridiculous words.

She took out a flattened packet of cigarettes from the pocket of her dress.

'You do smoke?' she asked.

'Of course,' I said. The blue vapour curled between us and then vanished into the air above our heads. The taste of it on my lips and in my nose brought incongruously the atmosphere of Sunday afternoons on the sand-dunes at school.

*

'I have,' she said, 'a long story to tell you. I don't see that it has anything to do with the murder you are investigating, though in the light it throws on my father's character and his affairs you may think it has. But if you listen to the end it must be because of your interest in me. And if at the end you want to leave me and do nothing for me I shan't be able to blame you. No, don't interrupt me.

'My mother, as perhaps you know, is dead,' she went on. 'When I left school I stayed at home to keep house for my father. He is at work all day and I was very lonely. The house, as you've seen from the outside, is decrepit and old-fashioned; inside it is just the same. All the afternoons I used to spend in the big, draughty sitting-room, staring at the crimson-paper walls and day-dreaming or reading one of a shelf of old novels that seemed to be part of the house – a book by Mrs Braddon or Mrs Humphrey Ward; romantic, high-toned, and serious. My head was full of nonsense – I see now.

'My father is not a talkative man, but at this time he became even quieter and more morose. I had the idea – encouraged by my reading – that a concealed sorrow was eating at his heart, or that there was some horrible secret in his life. One night – it was last winter, during the frightful February gales – he called me specially into the sitting-room, and made me sit down opposite him against the fire. He had a light-hearted air which I could see was unreal.

'"Rhoda," he said, "you are becoming a young woman. I am not very happy about the life you lead here with me. I believe you have a great career ahead of you – perhaps as the wife of some powerful man. You are very intelligent and you are not ill-looking, and when you grow out of this somewhat hazy stage of your existence I think you will reveal yourself to have great force of character."

'"I am quite happy with you here, Father," I said.

'"That may be," he replied, "but I am sure it is time that you began to move in a wider society. Tomorrow we are going to Checklock to visit a gentleman called Dr De'ath. He has asked us to his house for dinner. Dr De'ath has helped me very much in my business and I am under a great obligation to him. Tomorrow I want you to dress as well as you can and be very gracious to your host."

'The wind was still howling late the next afternoon when we went to Checklock. Dr De'ath's house was on the outskirts of the town in a road of houses, but detached and set among trees. In the hall, which was sombrely but sumptuously furnished, a man servant took our things and we were shown into a room lit only by candles and the flames of a large wood fire. The mellow light was reflected from brasses and the bindings of many books and the dull browns and greens of the tapestried walls. My excitement at all this new and rich existence was strikingly increased when I saw, coming towards us from the fire, the most handsome young man I have ever seen in my life. Could this be the person to whom my father owed so much?

'"Rhoda," said my father, "let me introduce you to Mr Brilliant. Mr Brilliant, this is my daughter Rhoda. Mr Brilliant is Dr De'ath's secretary."

'My feeling of disappointment was only momentary. Mr Brilliant shook hands with us and said that Dr De'ath would be down presently. We had sherry and chatted, and soon I began to feel that I had moved in such company all my life. Mr Brilliant's conversation was highly intelligent, but easy and witty. His face, in the soft light, seemed as though it had been carved out of old but flawless ivory; the short black curls of his hair fell over a forehead breathtaking in its height and serenity. Very soon Dr De'ath appeared, and against Mr Brilliant's beauty was put an ugliness so bizarre I can hardly describe it to you.

'Mr Brilliant was tall, but Dr De'ath taller. On top of his thin, sloping shoulders was an emaciated head completely devoid of hair. His skin was dark, but unhealthily dark – as though his face were turning rusty. And out of one side of his mouth projected not merely a yellowish fang but also, through some curious deformity, part of the gum from which it grew. His eyes were set in great pouches, puffed and scaly like the underside of a snake's head.

'And yet, after a little while, one began to forget his looks. He had a very gentle and quiet manner and a remarkable, deep voice whose fascination was rather increased by the lisp into which it was forced by his mouth's misshapenness. We went in to dinner – but there is no need for me to tell you anything more about that evening. It was the actors to whom I wished to introduce you – the drama came later.

'Nor need I tell you much of our next visit, which happened very soon after our first. At the end of dinner Dr De'ath had rung for his housekeeper to accompany me to the drawing-room, leaving the gentlemen with their port. On my way there with her I had a fancy to see the library and asked her to conduct me accordingly. She left me in a tall room, half lined with books and cabinets and with more books in great piles on the floor. I knew that one of Mr Brilliant's occupations was the indexing and arrangement of the library, and I was minded to see where and how Dr De'ath's secretary spent his days.

'I wandered among the books for a moment or two, and then put out my hand to lift one from a heap on the great table in the centre of the room. I had scarce grasped it when I heard a rapid step behind me, a quick breath – and then the volume was dashed from my hand. I turned round, horribly startled, to confront the flashing eyes and compressed lips of Mr Brilliant.

' "Whatever is the matter?" I cried.

'He averted his head, and said: "Surely it is too soon for you to look at the books."

' "I cannot understand what you mean, Mr Brilliant," I said.

' "Oh, Miss Savage," he breathed quickly, and then stopped abruptly.

' "What are you trying to tell me?" I said. I saw in his manner an exaggeration of the strangeness which I thought he had shown to me all that second evening.

' "How can I tell you anything?" There was something in his voice which was almost disgust.

' "Mr Brilliant," I exclaimed, "for pity's sake enlighten me. How – "

'But before I could utter another word I heard outside the door of the library the vibrant tones of Dr De'ath's voice. For no reason that I could see, I felt suddenly very frightened.

' "It is too chill in here for you, Miss Savage," said Dr De'ath, as his gaunt frame appeared. "Another night we will keep up the fire and you shall browse to your heart's content."

'As he gave me his arm to take me out, I glanced down to see the book which Mr Brilliant had so violently and unaccountably swept from my grasp. It was nothing more sinister than a volume of poems by the Jacobean poet, Donne.'

*

She stopped her narrative to take out and light another cigarette. I closed my mouth. It had been gaping, I realized, as I had sat watching her. Her pointed lemur's face was not turned fully towards me, and I saw the cheek in a severe but downy line, one distinguished eye and ear, and the piled brown hair. There was something fascinating and beautiful in the movement of her upper lip as she talked. I felt a causeless but delicious happiness.

*

'For several days,' she continued, 'I was uneasy. I could not imagine what meaning there had been in Mr Brilliant's words. Finally, I began to wonder whether behind our visits to Dr De'ath there were not some hidden and unpleasant motive. One night when my father and I were alone I led the conversation round to the doctor and his secretary and his great house.

' "Father, how is it," I asked, "that you have the entrée into such society?"

'He laughed in an embarrassed way. "Don't you think I am worthy of knowing anyone rich or powerful or intelligent?"

' "Of course – you are very nice. There is no one like you. But all the same, Dr De'ath and Mr Brilliant *are* exceptional creatures."

' "My dear," he said, reaching out his hand and drawing me on his knee, "Haven't you guessed that it is not entirely *my* qualities which admit us at Checklock?"

' "What do you mean?"

' "You, too, are an exceptional creature."

' "Nonsense, Father."

' "Oh yes; I am not the only one to think so." He turned his glance from me and stared abstractedly at the heavy red curtains. "Rhoda, you must begin to consider that some gentleman may one day ask you to marry him."

' "Marriage!" I exclaimed. "But I haven't considered it in the least."

' "You must consider it," he replied, gravely. "Have you never thought that there may be someone at Checklock who admires and respects you – and is attracted by you?"

'My heart started to pound, and I became the colour of the curtains. "But, Father – it's absurd," I stammered. "Mr Brilliant has not said a word to me – given no indication of a – a feeling for me other than that of one social acquaintance to another. I have only met him twice. I know nothing of him – except that he is cultured, handsome, and well-mannered. What grounds can you possibly have for imagining that he contemplates asking me to . . ." My voice died in a choke: a choke half of incredulity, half of exquisite joy as a hundred thoughts of the beautiful youth which I had hitherto forbidden myself coursed through my mind.

"There was a long silence, and then my father said softly: "Mr Brilliant is not the only gentleman at Checklock, nor has he the monopoly of culture and good manners there. And, after all, he is only a glorified servant. When I spoke of your possible marriage, Rhoda, I did not refer to Mr Brilliant." My father turned serious, anxious eyes to me. "It is Dr De'ath himself who loves you."

'I think that I must, as the image of the mottled face and fibrous body of Dr De'ath rose up in my imagination, have cried out aloud. I flew from my father's knee and stood facing him across the huge, old plush settee. I can still feel the sensation of its fabric on my fingertips.

' "No, no, no!" I kept moaning, until my father launched himself out of his chair and, leaning across, hit me sharply across the cheek. His lips were white with passion.

' "You little fool," he breathed, "Who are you to choose? Who are you to reject a rich and powerful suitor?"

' "I can never marry him." My lips formed these words, but I do not know whether I managed to make them audible.

' "I intend that you shall marry him."

'We stood glaring at each other, with the new, deep-seeing eyes of sudden enemies, for what seemed minutes. Then my father collapsed in his chair and buried his face in his hands. I made a little movement towards him and then checked myself. At last he lifted up a face stained with grief.

' "Rhoda," he said, brokenly, "I don't know what is to become of me."

'I said nothing.

' "I am in terrible trouble," he went on, dragging the words out of himself as though they were barbed. "I shall have to tell you. I had hoped that I should always be able to keep it from you. Rhoda, my life is ruled by Dr De'ath."

'At this my scalp crawled and I had a frightful premonition of a dark and inescapable fate.

' "Dr De'ath has a hold over me so grave," said my father, "that I can refuse him nothing. I am De'ath's creature. I must do everything he says. If I refuse he will divulge his information about me to the authorities and my life is at an end."

' "Father!" I cried. "What on earth is it that you've done?"

' "Do not ask me," he said. "It is something into which De'ath led me, but I alone bear the dreadful disgrace. It is something that I dare not divulge to another living soul. And now De'ath has said that you must become his wife."

'I could not reply. A lifetime of affection for and close contact with my father urged me to speak the consenting words which would bring an end to his torture – but I could not utter them. They were frozen in my throat by the icy memory of my father's blow and of Dr De'ath's visage.

' "Consider, Rhoda," my father was saying, "not only me, but yourself. As Mrs De'ath you would have power and money such as you have never dreamed of. You would have everything you want – clothes, jewels, books, cultivated society, the opportunity to travel..."

'I could say nothing. Gradually the torrent of his words declined to a trickle. An awful silence fell between us. The ticking of the clock in the corner was like the counting of a firing squad's commander. At length, nothing decided and each bearing a host of horrible thoughts within, we slunk separately to bed.'

*

'You may think,' said Rhoda Savage, 'that in our modern life all that happened could not possibly be so melodramatic as I have recounted it. I remember that such a thought passed through my mind as I lay sleepless in bed that night, about the terrible conversation with my father. I looked round the dark room and prayed for the light to come which, as I imagined, would give a commonplace and sane perspective to the events which had suddenly surrounded my life. But the day gave really no relief to the oppression which I felt in my heart and my stomach – felt so that I could not eat nor keep still. My father went out early to that work which I knew now must somehow be connected with Dr De'ath. I was left alone in the house. I had no friend to whom I could turn for help. Nor had I any prospect of making my own way in the world. As the hours wore on an idea, which at first had been but a germ, grew to dominate all my thought; I would go to Mr Brilliant, ask his advice, discover what lay at the bottom of that strange passage between us in the library and, if he would give it, enlist his aid. You may realize how materially helpless I was when I tell you that before I could make the journey to Checklock I had to take to a pawnbroker an old bracelet, my only possession of value – and that was but slight – which had belonged to my mother.

'For a long time I hovered round Dr De'ath's house, terrified of encountering its owner, yet longing more and more to unburden my soul to Mr Brilliant. Finally, I stole into the garden and from the cover of a grove, across a wide lawn, was able to watch the terrace at the back of it and a row of french windows standing open in the warm summer air. I could see, at times, Mr Brilliant's slim figure passing to and fro in the house; of the doctor there was no sign. I waited patiently until Mr Brilliant at last came on to the terrace, where he stood and lit a cigarette, his hair in the sunlight as blue as a starling's feathers. Only then did I dare to show myself. He started, crushed the cigarette under his heel, and walked rapidly across the lawn. I had gone back into the trees by the time he reached me; we went in the green, semi-gloom among the cool black trunks and the coins of light which spun down through the leaves.

' "Miss Savage," he said, "why did you not come to the house?" His manner had still that curious mixture of anxiety and frigidity which he had shown the last time we had met. But I think already he had seen in my face something of my trouble.

' "Is Dr De'ath in the house?" I asked quickly.

' "No," he said. "But I can get hold of him if you want to see him."

'I shuddered. "I do not want to see him."

' "Then you have come to see – me?"

' "Yes. I have come to ask you what you meant by the strange words you spoke to me in the library when I was last here."

' "Surely you understood quite clearly what I meant. In any case, why have you come to me in this – this furtive way?"

' "Because I need – most desperately – a friend. Mr Brilliant, why do you address me so coldly? When we first met you were kind, sympathetic. Now you are – "

' "Miss Savage, please, please control yourself." He was as agitated as I. "Is it possible that you are innocent?"

' "What in the name of pity do you mean?"

' "I am sorry," he said quickly, "to use such a word. Alas, I am not sure whether we are not talking at cross purposes. I must be frank with you, utterly frank. I must tell you everything."

'He took my arm and led me further into the trees and away from the house.

' "When I saw you first," he said, in a low voice, "I thought I had never seen one so unworldly, so fresh, so naturally spiritual. In this house, especially, you were like a first crocus against the sodden brown leaf-mould a winter old. I wondered what had brought you here. It was not long before I knew. One day Dr De'ath mentioned idly, as though it had been an appointment with his hatter, his forthcoming marriage. You must realize that to say that I was utterly shocked would be ludicrously to minimize my feelings."

' "But I don't realize," I cried. "It is true that for one of my age and position in society to marry Dr De'ath must occasion some surprise and comment – but to be more than utterly shocked! Surely you cannot know what I came here to tell you – that in my father's life is a dreadful secret, known to Dr De'ath; that Dr De'ath's threat to reveal the secret is the one and only reason why I should think of allying myself to him."

'Mr Brilliant groaned deeply. "My poor, troubled girl," he said at last, and took my hand gently and kept it in his. "Of course, I had no knowledge, no inkling, of this. I thought – forgive me – that you intended to marry De'ath of your own free will. That you desired it. That, belying your appearance, you were black, worldly, calculating. That you knew what a creature De'ath was and were prepared to take him in spite of what he was."

'A dread chill began to creep over me. "What do you mean," I whispered, "by *creature*?"

'Mr Brilliant dropped my hand and beat his forehead with his fist. "So that is it? You do not know De'ath? Oh, God!"

' "You are terrifying me. Tell me, only tell me."

' "If you do not know, I cannot tell you. Had you been a woman of twice your age, a woman of the world, a woman of experience, old in wickedness – still I could not possibly have told you. There is only one thing I can tell you, and that is, you must fly from this place, now, this very instant. Yes, that is all I can tell you – to put the utmost of space between yourself and De'ath."

'There were pearls of sweat on his marble brow. My heart was pounding.

' "You must tell me," I stammered, "you must tell me what it is that I have to run away from."

'During this passage we had moved unconsciously through the trees and had emerged at the edge of a little grassy space where at one end was a summer house and the other a statue. The statue, remarkable in a garden, was mounted on a huge plinth; it represented a girl or goddess, half reclining, with her arm round the neck of a kneeling man or god. The plinth and both the figures were stained and the nose of the male figure had been broken off. The whole object gave the scene something sinister and meaningful.

'Mr Brilliant said, "I cannot tell you. But I will say this. Listen to every word, for each one I utter must stand for a hundred I dare not. De'ath, as you may know, is a doctor of medicine. He does not practise now but once he was a very able surgeon. He is also an adept in magic. Do not laugh. There are books which treat of magic, not lightly or as a pursuit of savages, but as the study of intelligent, clever but distorted men. De'ath has all those books. I am not superstitious or credulous or uneducated and I tell you that there are magic practices which have results, awful results, in the material world we inhabit. De'ath is a combination of surgeon and magician. Those are both practical pursuits, but they need subjects. For surgery one requires bodies; for magic, souls."

'He grasped both my hands tight. "For the practical completion of his vile studies De'ath needs a human being. That being he must marry so that he can control her, keep her mouth for ever closed; so that her disappearance from the world will occasion as little notice as possible. For a hundred reasons. Now do you understand?"

'I could understand nothing except that I desired to run away. My lip was bleeding where I had bitten it to keep myself from crying out.

' "Rhoda," said Mr Brilliant, "I love you. I have loved you ever since I saw you first. I loved you even when I thought you a willing partner to De'ath's experiments. You must go away – will you go with me?"

'Among all my other emotions, somewhere there was found a place for the response to this declaration.

' "Yes," I cried. "Yes, I – "

'I had time for no more, for from the direction of the statue, as though that noseless, streaked figure had itself spoken, came a penetrating voice.

' "I think not," it said.

'Round the plinth tottered the cadaverous frame of Dr De'ath.'

*

'We were caught there in the glade,' said Rhoda Savage, 'as in a nightmare. Indeed, as Dr De'ath came forward and spoke again – calmly, easily; he completely dominated the scene – it seemed to me that everything had been ordained, and as soon as I felt that, part of me ceased to struggle. Mr Brilliant leapt forward and interposed himself between the doctor and me.

' "It is no use, De'ath," he said. "You cannot keep us here."

' "You are beside yourself, Brilliant," said Dr De'ath, dryly, looking over his shoulder at the statue. I followed his glance and saw, coming from behind the plinth, a short, thick-set man whom I recognized as the doctor's chauffeur.

'The struggle was soon over. Mr Brilliant was agile and courageous, but behind the chauffeur's brutality there was obviously a lifetime's training in pugilism. The chauffeur lugged the senseless body over his shoulder and set off in the direction of the house.

'I was numb. My body was set and trembling. I sensed rather than saw that Dr De'ath was at my side.

' "Miss Savage," he lisped. "I shall never forgive myself for leaving Brilliant unguarded. You will no doubt have guessed the truth about him. I heard you humouring him. He is a sad case.

' "At the Oxford of his time there was no more talented scholar, no young man of whom more was expected. An academic yet a supple mind, a forceful speaker, a subtle insight into politics, high-placed connexions, he looked forward to a great career. Alas, a hereditary taint of unsoundness in him grew to madness. His outburst of mania at length put an end to his studies. He was first brought to my notice in my professional capacity, and when I saw that his derangement had not altogether eclipsed his learning I suggested to his guardian that he lived with me and that side by side with the relationship of doctor and patient might run the equally calming relationship of tutor and student. For two years he has been my patient and my secretary. At first he was suspicious of me – he suffers, as you will have seen, from a persecution mania – but gradually I won his confidence. Until today I thought that I had won it completely, but I see now that behind the affectionate mask have boiled all the old insane delusions – the more furiously for being concealed. I can guess what ludicrous but foul insinuations he has made to you about me. I hope they did not occasion you too much distress. Now I do not know what to do with Brilliant. Clearly he must be restrained – you saw the savage attack just now on Bender. But here, in this house, it will be difficult to restrain him. And yet I would hate to send him to an asylum. Dear, dear. Come, Miss Savage, you are upset. Rest a while in the house, and then I will have Bender run you home. Of all the curses that alight on mankind, surely madness is the most dreadful. Poor Brilliant. Poor, poor Brilliant."

'Since I saw no alternative, I accompanied him into the house.'

*

At the word 'house' Rhoda Savage stopped speaking, took out another cigarette, and lit it. I waited for her to go on, but she didn't go on. She smoked furiously. And then it suddenly struck me that she had come to the end of her story.

'And who – ' I stopped, because my throat was full of emotion or phlegm, cleared it, and started again. 'And who was *really* mad?'

'I don't know,' she said, in a high voice that hovered on the edge of tears.

There was another silence and then my words came in a rush.

'But what happened? What are you doing here? Where is Brilliant?'

'Mr Brilliant is a prisoner at Dr De'ath's. I have never seen him since that day in the garden.'

'And De'ath's threat to your father?'

'I am marrying Dr De'ath.'

We had been on the heath so long that the sun had gone down and the houses on the perimeter were beginning to be lost in the violet haze of twilight. Trails of mist were creeping close to the grass.

'How can you possibly marry him?' I said.

'How can I possibly not? You saw my father in court – didn't you notice that he was a nervous wreck? To refuse to marry Dr De'ath would simply be signing my father's death warrant.'

'But –'

'Don't you understand?' she cried. 'I have been over the thing time and time again – from every angle. I have thought and felt about it until I am sick of thought and feeling. That is all finished with.'

'Can't you go to the police?'

She laughed without amusement. 'I have been to the police. Oh, they were very helpful. "Dr De'ath," they said, "is a well-known and most respectable medical practitioner. He has a secretary named Brilliant who is also, they understand, his patient. There have been no complaints by or on behalf of Mr Brilliant – why should there be? How can it possibly be a case for police inquiries? Has any crime been committed? You must have been wrongly informed, Miss Savage." they said.'

'Haven't you tried to see Brilliant?' I said.

Rhoda Savage leaned towards me and clutched my hand; she was warm and her nails were sharp – the lemur's little claws. 'That is it, Frederick,' she said, vehemently. 'That is it. That is what I want you to do.'

'Me?' I said. When she had used my name a delicious but alarming metaphorical hand had scraped down my spine.

'You are free to go away now, if you want to. Just get up and walk away. You need not stay any longer.'

I did not go away and she went on. 'It's grotesque, isn't it? You must think that. We are strangers and yet you know more about me than anyone else in the world.'

'I said before that I don't feel that we are strangers.'

'I don't feel that either. I didn't feel it even when I first saw you in the garden. That's why I asked you here. And because I am desperate.'

And now, for the first time, a little cough of a sob escaped her, as involuntarily as a hiccup, but she quickly continued speaking: 'You are solving the Preece murder. I don't know whether all I've told you has anything to do with that; if it has, that is a good reason why you should help me, isn't it?'

I nodded.

She said slowly and haltingly: 'But there's another reason, Frederick. Don't think me foolish. You might want to help me because of me.'

I felt that I might be about to blush – both for her and for myself – and was glad of the twilight. 'Rhoda,' I said, and as I said it the same frightful hand went along my back. 'Of course it would be because of you.' Instead of being ironical and hypocritical my words became, in a surprising and unmeant way, sincere. And, therefore, silly. She was a dreadful influence. The mist crept round us, chill and smelling of metal.

'What do you want me to do?' I asked, at last.

'Mr Brilliant,' she said. 'He is the key to it all. If he is mad, then that is the end of everything and I must go through with what I have to go through. But if he is sane, then it is Dr De'ath who is mad. Mr Brilliant must be set free.'

Her demands kept slapping against me, like waves against a sea-wall. I felt half hypnotized. 'Yes,' I said, 'that is the point. He must be let out. But how?'

'I don't know,' she said.

'I'll get him out,' I said.

She smiled, a little wanly. 'I knew you would. Fate sent you to me.'

'Don't you think I can do it?'

'It is very dangerous. There is not only Dr De'ath, there is Bender.'

'I can do it.'

*

Only a moment later, it seemed, I was in the train for Checklock – though we had walked to the edge of the heath, and in the shadow of a willow-tree by a pond discussed plans, and she had written De'ath's address in my notebook. But with her time ceased to have its normal value. I looked at my ghostly reflection in the carriage window, read over and over again her careless, unformed, and charming writing, swallowed continually at the pulse of excitement in my throat – but all was without reality. I thought of the meeting we had arranged for the next day, and imagined what we would talk about. I tried to picture what her face was like and could not. During the whole of the hour's journey I was in a fever and in that state I was thrown out into Checklock's High Street, among the newspaper boys and the neon lighting and the crowds going to the cinema.

At that moment I had a partial return of sanity, remembered that I had not been home all day, and went into a telephone box. Mrs MacBean answered.

'Can I speak to my father, Mrs Mac?' I said.

'He's no' in.'

'Where's he gone?'

'To the cottage.'

That was excellent; it meant he wouldn't be back until Monday.

'Did he ask about me?'

'Aye. He said were ye no' living here the noo.'

'Oh,' I said. 'Well, I shall be late home tonight.' I thought of Bender and said: 'I may not be home at all – I'm going to see some friends.'

'What will I do with the pigeons I've got for your supper, Master Frederick?'

After some inconclusive cross-talk I put back the receiver, went into the street, and asked a policeman the way to the road in which De'ath's house was. Then I bought a pork pie and bar of chocolate and ate them as I walked along, though my stomach was too fluttery for hunger.

Soon the street lamps became fewer, trees appeared, the moon (near and very yellow and crumbly) became noticeable and only occasionally did I pass a human being. My footfalls echoed down the still-paved but quiet road. I could not help thinking how side by side with modern civilized activity existed this other state of life, where the symbols of nature were still operative, and the things men had made – houses, lamps, telephone wires – took on the quality of nature and at night became sinister. In this world existed Dr De'ath.

I must have walked for over a mile before I came to the street in which he lived. Rhoda Savage had described its location very inaccurately – I had to ask twice again before I found it. It rose steeply from the road I was in; it was ill-lit, and trees obscured the houses. I leaned against a wall at the bottom and tried to think. It was hopeless; rope-ladders, broken windows, and bludgeons whirled in my brain. There was only one thing for it – to make a plunge, whatever sort of belly-flop it was.

As I leaned there I heard someone coming softly down the hill. My heart started to beat even faster and I looked round furiously and in vain for somewhere to hide. But it was madness simply to stand there, so I bent down and started untying and tying up my shoelace. Very soon I saw, out of the corner of my eyes, skirts, and skirts so long that they could only belong to a very old lady. My heart went back to that apprehensive pulsing that since I had met Rhoda Savage was its norm, and after a decent interval I straightened up. When I looked round the old lady had disappeared and so I went on cautiously up the hill. There was a fragrance in the air, as of cigars, which I only half-noticed at the time, but afterwards recalled so vividly.

De'ath's house was called Grangemere. I found the name threequarters erased on a gate that leaned drunkenly. I was using my electric torch – there was no street lamp within fifty yards. I did not trust to the gate being silent so I vaulted over it, and then listened carefully. The night was utterly quiet. When I had gone a few steps up the path, the house came into view, crudely and poorly illumined by the moon. I had a curiously violent shock; it was very much smaller than I had imagined it. At one corner was a mid-Victorian turret, and along the first floor ran a wooden balcony which even in that light I could see was broken down.

The moonlight glittered on a broken attic window panel. I was greatly tempted to hop back over the gate and shine my torch on the name again to make absolutely sure of it.

There were no lights at the windows. I crept round the house to discover what rooms were occupied at the back. I found myself fighting my way through a tangle of bushes. There was a strong smell of rotting vegetation. When I came round to the other side of the house I could see that that, too, was in darkness. Even then, though a pulse started to hammer in my stomach as well as my chest, I did not really think that anything was wrong. Images rose to my mind of a madman in a black room, filthy on his straw, or of a man as sane as I, bound and gagged and gazing hopelessly into the darkness. And then I had a sudden feeling of exultation; was the whole thing going to be easy after all? Was this the very opportune moment? I wriggled back through the bushes. Waiting for me on the path was a little old woman.

*

She was standing under a tree, so I could hardly see anything of her. Perhaps I shouldn't even have known it was a woman if it hadn't been for the incident at the bottom of the hill.

'Oh,' I said straight away, in a voice which I did not recognize as mine, 'I'm afraid I'm getting lost – missed the path completely. Do you happen to know if Mrs MacBean lives here?'

'I am Mrs MacBean,' said the old lady. 'What do you want?'

It was then, I suppose, that I knew the game was up. But I struggled on.

'Mr French's housekeeper?'

'Yes,' said the inexorable voice.

I laughed unconvincingly. 'I didn't recognize your voice, Mrs MacBean. You remember me, don't you?'

'No. Who are you?'

It was terrible. I turned and made a sudden, desperate dash for the gate. The old woman was astonishingly agile; she took a couple of nimble strides and thrust out her leg in my path. I went rolling among the weeds and the bushes, winded. A second later I felt a knee in my back and two pressing hands at the back of my neck which kept my face half-buried in the moss of the path.

'Who are you?' said the old lady again.

'Powder,' I gasped. 'Powder. John Powder.' It was a situation reminiscent of my earlier schooldays, when I was sometimes at the mercy of unpleasant and larger boys.

'What do you want here?' said the old lady.

'Bender,' I said, through dirt. 'Mr Bender. A message from his sister.'

The pressure of the hands increased and I realized that from the creature on top of me I could expect not even the mercy of a bully. I had an awful ten seconds of panic. I could not breathe and I thought I was going to die.

'What do you want? What do you want?' I heard the voice saying, like a voice behind the roaring and scraping of an ancient gramophone record. I threshed wildly with my legs and tore at the path with my nails. The hands relaxed a little and I was able to cough out one word.

'Brilliant.'

And then I felt a dull, heavy blow on that part of my head out of which my neck grew. A shower of sparks flew into the blackness of my eyes and I became unconscious.

*

I dreamt that I was at school. Unaccountably, I was lying across one desk with my head in the interior of another. The lid of the latter desk was pressed down excruciatingly on the back of my neck. At the front of the class was Admiral Crowborough-Crow reading from a green-covered book. 'The features,' intoned the Admiral,

> *'The features in their private dark*
> *Are formed of flesh, but let the false day come*
> *And from her lips the faded pigments fall,*
> *And mummy cloths expose an ancient breast.'*

Behind his head was an ill-lit corner of ceiling with a cobweb across it. 'So you're awake. Who are you?' said the Admiral.

'Oh, my head,' I groaned. And then I realized that the ceiling was not a part of the school at all, but in a strange room where I was lying on the floor. And the Admiral had turned horribly into an old woman, yellowly illuminated and that it was she who was chanting:

> 'Should lanterns shine, the holy face,
> Caught in an octagon of unaccustomed light,
> Would wither up, and any boy of love
> Look twice before he fell from grace.'

I heard myself groan again, and then once more the ceiling was the school ceiling. Ronnie Reeves came up to me and sat on the lid of the desk my head was in. Luckily, before the pain became too much to bear, I fainted.

5 SUNDAY, 9 *September*

WHEN I became conscious again there was no lamplight and no old lady. I was still on the floor. One arm, through lying on it, had become numb and spongy and curiously limp. When I put my hand to the back of my head to find out what was ticking there, I encountered an alarmingly big and painful lump.

The room I was in was large. An assortment of blankets and travelling rugs were tacked up at the window, but at their edges was a burr of light. It was morning then. My dreams were still so vivid and the night before had been so grotesque that it was difficult to adjust myself to what was now undoubtedly reality. I got up and tottered to the window. Lifting an edge of blanket, I could look out over an untidy garden and then over a little wood towards a great sweep of downs, mistily green in the low sun. The room was evidently on the first or second floor.

I realized suddenly that I had to get out of the place, and rushed madly to the door. It was locked, of course. I began to prowl about, massaging my arm, a dreadful feeling of fear growing inside me. I started talking to myself. 'What am I going to do?' I said. 'What on earth am I going to do?'

In time I become rather more normal. I tried to fit the old woman into Dr De'ath's household; I tried to reconcile Rhoda Savage's account of the splendid house at Checklock with the neglected garden below and this filthy and half-furnished room. It occurred to me for the first time – which shows how her personality had overpowered me – that her story had been very highly coloured and the characters as monstrous as those in a Brontë novel. And what I had found the house to be like in reality would be paralleled by the real characters of its occupants. De'ath would be a grubby, superannuated general practitioner; Brilliant a gibbering, moronic ex-clerk; Bender a rough but not unamiable odd-job man. Perhaps, anyway, getting things into this sort of perspective gave me fresh confidence; if it were only ordinary people I had to tackle, I knew I could tackle them successfully. Most people are bigger fools than one is oneself. I went to the window to open it and to look for a convenient drainpipe. Before I could get to it I heard the lock click and someone opened the door.

The window coverings kept most of the light out: I could only dimly see the old woman who stood in the doorway. Even so, she had a very strange look. She could not have been more than four feet and a few inches and she had a bowed appearance. On her large head was a large hat, like a melon, pulled down over her eyes. In her hand she held what looked very much like a knife. The feeling of fear began to grow again at my middle.

She was still at her questionings of the night before. 'What have you come here for, John Powder?' she said. 'If that is your real name.'

'Certainly it's my real name,' I said with much swallowing of nervous saliva.

'Well, what do you want?' she asked again. She had a cracked voice which descended to a baritone's range on certain words.

'What are you keeping me here for?' I said, with a perkiness that astonished me.

'Shut up,' she screeched, 'and answer me.'

I decided to tell her something of the truth, and unconsciously walked a few paces towards her. Instantly she brandished what she had in her right hand: it was certainly a knife. 'Keep away,' she cried, 'keep away.'

I retreated far into the room, and the ensuing dialogue was rather ludicrously conducted over a distance of about ten yards.

'I am a friend of Mr Brilliant,' I began.

'Liar,' said the old woman.

I tried again. 'I am a friend of a friend of Mr Brilliant, and that friend asked me to help him.'

'What is the friend called?'

'I'm afraid I can't tell you that. You see – '

The old woman fairly danced with rage. 'Can't tell me, can't tell me! I'll cut you up, you young fool. Cut you up without any compunction. Who is this Bender you talked of last night?'

It was a mad conversation. 'Bender? Well, you should know.'

'I'm asking you.'

'He is the chauffeur here. Dr De'ath's chauffeur.'

'Dr De'ath? Who is Dr De'ath?'

It struck me then that either I had come to the wrong house or that the old woman was another lunatic patient of the doctor's. 'Dr De'ath is Mr Brilliant's employer, of course.'

'Oh, God! Oh, God!' groaned the old woman. 'Now look here. I have a knife and I'm desperate. Tell me this, and I want the truth: are you from the police?'

'No, no,' I said, and put all the sincerity I could into my voice. I hoped she could detect it.

She muttered a bit to herself and then said aloud: 'I shall be back, and when I come back I want the truth.'

And with that she banged the door and locked it. I sat down in the middle of the floor, put my throbbing head in my hands, and wept.

*

It was half past seven when she left me; she did not come back until after one o'clock. During most of that time I thought about ways of escape, and even tried a few. It took me nearly an hour to open the window; I dare not make any noise, and it had clearly never been opened for a generation. Old paint had jammed the sash against the frame and the cords were broken. When at last I had it open and I could look out there was no nearby drainpipe and the basement area was a dizzy distance below. There was another floor above me, so access to the roof was impossible. I then ransacked the room for something with which to force the door and another something with which to crown the old woman if I got the chance. The only articles of furniture were a broken bentwood chair and an old iron bed littered with grey sheets. I disintegrated the chair and made myself a handy club from one of the legs. The door was of a Victorian solidity and could not be opened with anything I had available. With my club across my breast I lay on the repugnant bed like the effigy on a crusader's tomb. I was bored, and, what was worse, hungry and thirsty. I longed for the reappearance of the old woman, who would, I thought, bring me at least a cup of water. I thought of Rhoda Savage. I never once thought of the Preece murder case.

At last I heard footsteps outside the door, and the old woman's voice. She evidently had her mouth at the keyhole.

'Powder,' she said, 'are you ready to tell me why you're here?'

I got off the bed and buttoned the club inside my jacket in case she was peeping.

'I've always been ready,' I shouted.

'I don't want to hear anything more about Bender and De'ath,' she said, sulkily. 'I want the truth.'

'I'll tell you the truth. And I'm hungry and thirsty.'

'I'll bring you some food when you've told me why you're here. Are the curtains down?'

'No.'

'Well, pull them down. And stay by the window. And no monkey tricks; I can see you through the keyhole.'

I pulled the curtains down, but did not remain by the window. 'They're down,' I called and went and stood where the door would hide me when it opened. If she could see the window through the keyhole, then she was a witch and capable of looking round corners. I drew out the club from my jacket.

The door unlocked and opened cautiously. Into the dim light swam the melon hat. I hit it as hard as I could with the chair leg. In fiction such an action would have caused the wearer of the hat to sink without a groan to the ground. In reality the old woman emitted a frightful bellow, turned round the door, and gave me a great kick in the stomach. As I went down I clutched at her skirts and we went rolling over the floor together. But I was already finished; all my energies and intelligence were concentrated on the problem of getting my stomach to expand again so to be able to take a breath. Just as I began to see how (by drawing my knees up to my chin and keeping very still) this might be achieved, the old woman scrambled to her feet and gave me another kick – this time, since my stomach was badly placed, in the kidneys. She was a formidable old woman.

When I was able to interest myself again in the outer world, I saw that she was sitting on the bed. She still had a knife in her hand. In the struggle I must have rolled on the knife, because I felt a sharp burning along my cheek and when I touched it my hand came away bloody. Or perhaps she had pinked me warningly. I began to be frightened again.

'You young devil,' she was saying.

I propped myself on one elbow and kneaded my stomach with my free hand. She seemed not to be at all affected by the blow with the chair leg. Of course, the extraordinary hat had protected her. I had simply knocked it a little cockeyed. Knocked it so that it now shadowed her face rather less and revealed some hair which, curiously, was black. Her nose, I could see, was snub and her jaw was very heavy for a woman. And then, without any effort and with hardly any surprise (just as long ago in my infancy I had suddenly known that there was no Father Christmas), I realized that she was not a woman at all, but a man in woman's clothes.

*

'Well, are you ready to talk?' said the person sitting on the bed.

I kneaded and dabbed alternately; they had become reflex actions while my mind raced away trying to deal with the new situation. Behind its obscurity I felt instinctively that a blinding light was about to break. I plunged towards it through the darkness.

I said: 'You're a man, aren't you?'

The person hastily pulled the hat forward, and then swore and pushed it back so far that it fell on the bed. He wiped his brow delicately with the hand that held the knife.

'Well, since you're here and I shall have to watch you, there's no sense in keeping up this ridiculous disguise. You twigged me all the time, I suppose?'

'All the time,' I said.

'Even in the street?'

'I wasn't quite sure in the street.'

'That's something, anyway,' he said. 'Putting these clothes on is the only way I can get any fresh air at all, of course. And then I can only go out at night, and in the quiet streets round here. Let's have some light on the subject.'

He went to the window and jammed up the curtaining. The sunlight lit his curly black hair, his immense head, his sallow dwarf's face which had a curious fixity of expression. I had simply no time to reason out how it was that I had done accidentally what Toller and the C.I.D. had failed to do (that is to say, found Elshie) because he was questioning me again.

'Now,' he said, 'who are you?'

I groaned and massaged my stomach more desperately while I tried to think who I ought to be. He watched me dispassionately and said:

'You asked for it. You're lucky really. I might have killed you instead of kicking you.'

I groaned again and bent my head down, but he came again with the question.

'Who are you, damn you?' he said, fretfully.

It was no use; I still did not know, so I said: 'Rhoda Savage told me to come.' I waited for him to kick me again and ask who Rhoda Savage was, but instead he jumped to his feet and went stumping angrily about the room, saying: 'I might have known it! I might have known it!' His little figure with the skirts up to his armpits looked exactly like something out of a circus. I began to feel safer.

'She thought I could help you,' I ventured.

He swore horribly. 'What in heaven's name made her do it? How did she get to know where I was?' He muttered to himself for some time. And then he turned to me suspiciously.

'Are you one of Rhoda's boy friends?'

'Yes,' I said, and felt suddenly sad.

'Did she tell you why I was hiding here? I suppose you've gathered that I'm not dressed like this in this Godforsaken hole for amusement.'

I went warily. 'She didn't tell me anything about you. It was really Mr Brilliant she wanted me to help.'

The dwarf came and peered into my face. 'Oh, it was Mr Brilliant, was it?' he said.

'Yes, where is he?'

The dwarf laughed tonelessly. 'You've come to the wrong place.' And then he became menacing again. 'I want the truth from you. You understand that, I hope.'

'I understand.'

'And how were you to assist Mr Brilliant?'

'By helping him to escape.' I refrained from saying anything about De'ath.

'I see. The girl's mad,' said the dwarf. 'Mad to tell you all this. I can't understand it.'

'Is this house called Grangemere?' I asked him.

'Of course it's called Grangemere. Didn't you see it on the gatepost?'

I couldn't understand it either.

I said: 'You said you'd bring me something to eat and drink.'

'We'll both have something to eat and drink,' said the grotesque creature.

*

When he came back, half an hour later, carrying a tray laden with food, a bottle, and a jug of water, he had removed his skirt and blouse and was revealed as wearing a dark blue shirt, and a piccalilli-coloured tweed jacket, his little billiard-table legs in corduroy trousers. I think while he was out of the room he must have had a shave – his swarthy cheeks were mottled with talcum powder; they went curiously with his blue-rimmed fingernails. He handed me a plate on which there was a slug of corned beef, a hunk of bread, and an enormous, vinegar-dripping onion. He had a duplicate plate for himself. Since I had destroyed the chair, I ate on the floor. He sat on the bed using his sheath-knife to cut his onion and spear the corned beef. I used my fingers, and made nearly as loud smacking noises as he did.

'Whisky?' he said, with his mouth full.

'Water, please.'

He poured me a glass of water and himself two inches of whisky. When we had finished the corned beef we had some cheese; it was leathery, rather sweaty Empire Cheddar, but it tasted wonderful. Then the dwarf poured himself some more whisky and lay back on the bed, picking his teeth with the point of his knife. I made myself as comfortable as I could against the wall. The dwarf lit a cigar.

'You're rather a pretty boy, aren't you?' he remarked suddenly.

He was such a ridiculous figure that I could not blush. 'That isn't the adjective I would use,' I said.

'Oh, come,' he said, 'you must know that you're pretty. Didn't Rhoda tell you, anyway?'

I blushed then.

'It is a great pity that you've got yourself into this mess,' he went on. 'I don't know what will happen to you.'

He was ridiculous but infinitely unpleasant – unpleasant because it was clear that we had not a single feeling in common. And I knew, as I watched him sipping his whisky, that, fundamentally, I was frightened of him.

'What will happen to me when?' I said.

'You don't think we can stay here for ever, do you?' He waved his hand at the haze of his cigar smoke so as to get a better look at me. 'You are a pretty and deep boy. How much did Rhoda tell you?'

'She didn't tell me anything. I wish she had, and then I wouldn't have come. I had a curious dream last night,' I said. I could think of nothing else that would change the conversation. 'Someone was intoning verse. And when I woke up it was still being intoned. It couldn't have been you, could it?'

'Why don't you think so?' said the dwarf.

'I regard you rather as a man of action.'

The dwarf seemed to be very pleased. I think the whisky was

mellowing him. 'So I am, so I am. But an intellectual one. You are an intellectual too, I see. But hardly a man of action as well – not a successful one, anyway.'

'Who is your favourite poet?' I asked politely.

'You heard me quoting him last night. Did you like it?'

'I only heard it through a dream.'

'That is how one should hear all poetry. Poetry is only an elaboration of images from the subconscious.'

'Matthew Arnold didn't think so.'

'Throw away all that Matthew Arnold stuff, boy. Poetry has been liberated since his day. Listen to this.'

The dwarf leaned forward, and waving his cigar rhythmically, recited the following lines in a voice so consciously modulated and beautiful that I could have kicked him:

> *'Caught in the fig-bright mountain of his breast*
> *The net of blood pulsed, slowly like a star,*
> *And burning in the sunset for a crest*
> *The blackened crack of Jack-a-Christ's cracked spar.*
> *O double father in the womb of gales!*
> *His hair bent backward in a knotty cross,*
> *My ten dead fingers like ten dead lank sails*
> *Chained in the glassy bubbled calm of loss.'*

When I thought he had finished, I said: 'Very impressive. Very impressive indeed.'

He relaxed and took a pull at his cigar. 'Whose work, do you think?'

'Well,' I said, 'at school I am rather bogged down in the Matthew Arnold period. My form master, Mr Waggon, doesn't care for any poet later than Clough – and no novelist later than Jane Austen. So I'm afraid I don't know the moderns very well.'

'I wrote it,' said the dwarf. 'It was a mad world I was in.

'I am,' he went on, between sips of whisky, 'one of the Armageddon Group of poets.'

He paused for a comment from me, and I said, weakly, 'Really.'

'Didn't you ever read *The New Revelation*? That was an anthology we brought out soon after the movement started. It did more to enlarge the frontiers of poetry and the frontiers of the individual spirit than anything in the last fifty years. Poetry had become aridly realistic, sterilely commonsensical – we did away with all that. After *The New Revelation* no young poet could write in the same way again.'

*

The afternoon wore on. After a while I accepted a glass of whisky and water; I thought it might numb me a little to the stream of verse, unknown names, Soho public-houses, bi-annual periodicals, that flowed from the dwarf ever more quickly as the whisky coursed through his veins. In the end I was a little drunk I think; he was quite drunk. He came and sat by me on the floor. Black hair grew out of his nostrils and ears; the whites of his eyes were bloodshot, the pupils a strange light grey. His face was so ugly and so expressionless that I could have believed it was a mask. He put his arm round my shoulder.

'Look, John,' he said, 'I must tell you this. I've been boasting. Forget it. Forget I told you I was a good poet. I may be a decent poet, I may be very decent indeed. But I'm not good, not by the highest standards.'

'I think you are good,' I said, edging away from him.

He clutched me desperately. 'I'm not good, John. No, I'm not good. I'm a failure. It's swell of you to say I'm good, but I'm a failure. Listen, this is in absolute confidence – you'll be shocked but I've got to tell you. I couldn't have you know me as you do without knowing this. Once upon a time I nearly went to prison, John.'

'That doesn't make any difference to me.'

'It's swell of you to say that, John.' His voice broke. 'I've killed my work with my life. One slip when I was a boy – not much older than you, John – and you see where it's landed me. Hiding here, like a hunted fox. . . . They'll get me away, of course. They'll get me away tomorrow. But what a place for an artist to start a new life in. . . .'

My heart leapt. 'Where?' I said. I was certain that it was the arm of Preece's murderer round my neck.

He didn't answer me; he was maundering off on another tack. 'Perhaps, though, a new country ... I might be as good as Jones. John, do you know Gryfydd Jones's poetry? Do you know it?'

'Afraid not.'

'He's good. I'm decent. He's good. Listen to this:

> *'O consultations of fishes in the ocean's blue*
> *Tabernacles and my heart –'*

He stopped. 'How does it go?' He scrambled to his feet. 'I'll get my copy of *The New Revelation*. You must hear it.' He tottered to the door on his grotesque legs; he had not far to fall I thought. In spite of his fuddledness he locked the door behind him.

I rushed to the window, opened it, and once again looked for a possible way out. It was no use. I pulled at the door until my arms ached. I even put my head into the fireplace and peered up the chimney. I had to get away. Most incongruously, I heard in the distance a church bell announcing Evensong. Once more I felt like weeping.

He was back again very soon with the book. He locked the door behind him and dropped the key in a side pocket of his jacket. He came very close to me and thrust the book under my nose. *The New Revelation*, it said in sophisticatedly childish letters on the dust jacket. Under this title was a drawing of a bleeding heart and so on, and then a list of contributors. From this list a name jumped out and hit me between the eyes – OSCAR BRILLIANT.

I pointed to it with a rather shaky finger. 'I know this name,' I said.

'Of course you know it, John dear,' said the dwarf. 'That is my name. Didn't you believe me when I told you I was a poet? But *I'm* only a decent one. I want you to hear the work of a good one.' He rifled through the pages of the book. 'Here we are. Gryfydd Jones. Listen:

> *'O consultations of fishes in the ocean's blue*
> *Tabernacles and my heart still swimming over*
> *The lucent fathoms of my youth ...'*

I heard no more. Oscar Brilliant, Oscar Brilliant, beat in my brain. I had a totally disturbing sense of horrible confusion and clear understanding. Suddenly I was conscious that the dwarf had stopped reading.

'Well?' he said, smiling drunkenly.

'Oh, superb,' I said. 'Simply superb.'

'What about Matthew Arnold now?'

'Out. Completely out.'

'This is all a new revelation to you, isn't it?'

'Yes,' I said. 'A new revelation. But, Mr Brilliant – you've left the door open. Ought you to do that?'

He turned his great silly head in the direction of the door; the whisky had slowed up his reactions and I had just time to flash my arm across the floor, seize the chair-leg and knock the bottom of his skull, before he could realize what I was doing. There was no hat to protect him this time and he toppled forward until his snub nose was made more snub against the pages of *The New Revelation*. Tremulously, I thrust my hand in his pocket, got the key, ran to the door, opened it, and flew down the corridor towards a staircase.

I shall never forget the atmosphere of the house that Sunday evening; the last shafts of sunlight caught on walls from which the paper hung in mouldering strips like tropical vegetation, the dust which my frantic footsteps raised, the grimy green paintwork, the heavy plaster of the ceilings, and, as I came rattling down the last flight of stairs into the hall, an alarming, almost life-sized marble of a nymph holding a torch aloft. When I reached the front door, through the half-stained glass door of a vestibule, I found boards nailed across it. Foolishly I started pulling at them – until I realized that the door had not been opened for years, and that the dwarf must use another one. As I turned and was coming out of the vestibule I heard him descending the stairs.

I went back and flattened myself behind the door of the vestibule. Through the glass I could watch the staircase; it was blood-red. The adjacent strip of glass allowed me to see the marble nymph, changed to green. A blue corridor like a grotto ran from the bottom of the staircase to the back of the house.

In a moment or two the crimson dwarf came hurtling down the stairs; the knife in his hand was crimson, too. I should have taken the knife. For an instant he turned a ghastly green and I thought he was coming straight towards me. And then, with a sense of relief which drained all the blood out of my legs, I saw his blue back disappear down the corridor. He must have thought I had gone for the back entrance.

I tiptoed over the bare, screaming boards of the hall back up the stairs. It was a retreat, but all I could do. Half-way across I remembered I could take my shoes off; the worst moments of the whole affair were when I stood in the middle of the suddenly gigantic and exposed floor and struggled with a knot in a lace. But at last I was padding up the staircase.

After a couple of trials, I found a room on the first floor which looked out over the front garden and the door of which had a lock and key. I locked myself in. I got my notebook, tore out a sheet, and wrote on it this message: ELSHIE IS AT GRANGEMERE, DOWNS ROAD, CHECKLOCK, AND LEAVES MONDAY. I'M THERE TOO. FREDERICK FRENCH.

I folded the sheet and put it in one of the small envelopes which, in childish but fortunate imitation of Dr Thorndyke, I had been carrying about ever since the case began. On the envelope I wrote: INSPECTOR TOLLER, C.I.D., NEW SCOTLAND YARD, LONDON, SW and over that VITAL: PLEASE POST OR DELIVER. I weighted the envelope with part of the cover of the notebook, and then sealed it up. I even had a half-penny stamp, so I put that on it.

Even before I started to struggle with the window I heard the dwarf again. He must have found the back door still locked and so have known I had not left the house. I could distinguish remote bellowings and stampings. I was frightened. I hit round the window frame until the ball of my thumb was the colour of a boiled lobster. And then Brilliant was outside the door. The window went up with a great screech. Brilliant started pounding on the door.

'Are you in there, Powder?' he shouted.

The glass on this side of the house was so weather-stained that I had not been able to see out of the room clearly until the window was open. The trees which lined the front garden wall were very close, their tops higher than the window. I took a deep breath, got Toller's letter between my first and second fingers, and, leaning far out of the window, I skimmed it, as though it were a cigarette card in those games I used to play in my extreme youth, as hard as I could.

'Let me in, Powder, and then I'll murder you.'

The letter whirled whitely against the just-darkening sky and rode over the green bank of the trees as gracefully and easily as a floating gull over a wave. All my hopes went with it; they were not very lively. Still leaning out of the window, I started to shout.

'Help!' I roared. 'Help, help, help!'

When I stopped for breath, I heard at the door a dreadful prising and cracking sound. The ground was too far away to jump for it; again there were no handy drainpipes. With one eye on the door I shouted again. Sitting sideways on the sill I could see through a gap in the trees to what must have been the other side of the road. There seemed to be no houses opposite at all; only the swelling contours of the downs again, and on them a grandstand and a line of white rails, which would be Checklock Racecourse. There was little chance of my shouts ever being heard, let alone acted upon.

When the door flew open and Brilliant burst into the room he had his knife in his teeth, like a Christmas play pirate, because his hands were still occupied with a long and heavy-looking poker. But there was nothing entertaining about him. My upraised arm took some of the force of his blow off my head, but not enough to prevent me from being knocked, once more, completely unconscious.

*

It was all as it had been before. I felt someone trying to drag me up the steep sides of a black pit. Again and again I fell back. When at last I struggled out, I saw, sitting on the bed and gazing through the window at the moon, Brilliant's hunched figure. This time he was not chanting poetry; he had a fearful and agonized look. I remember thinking that no one could have heard my shouts, and

I had a visual image of my little letter to Toller lying trampled and ignored in Downs Road. A continuous throbbing lifted my head up and down on the floor. I looked into the pit with fear and a few moments later slid into its depths again.

6 MONDAY, 10 *September*

IT was light when I awoke. I felt terrible. My watch had stopped, but I judged it to be very early morning. Brilliant was not in the room; there was a row of crushed cigarette stubs like a row of bad teeth along the window-ledge. It was raining outside: the sky was a dark grey monotone, the line of the downs invisible, the trees in the garden a dripping and electric green. There was somehow in the air a sense of desperation and danger; the comic boredom of Sunday had all gone and I felt nothing like it would return. What was to happen to me? Though Brilliant (I felt sure) did not appreciate how much I knew, yet he knew I knew too much for his safety. I then thought that I was going to be sick and so I opened the window and leaned out. The cool air and the rain revived me a little and I wasn't sick. I turned tremblingly back into the room. The best I could hope for was that Brilliant would make his getaway and leave me in the house. If he would only do that I would think later of how I was to escape from this locked room. As for the case, it could go hang. All I wanted was to be able to sit in my own room again and see the lamps in the square and to have a bath and to drink cup after cup of Earl Grey tea and to read and talk with my father.

And yet I knew that even though I got out of this place unharmed my life would never be the same again. For underneath the anxiety about Brilliant was a deeper and permanent ache which had as its stabbed centre she whose face I had tried, since I left her, in vain to imagine. Only her name had any reality for me, and I kept saying it – Rhoda, Rhoda, Rhoda – like an incantation of dubious efficacy. I could not even imagine that I had ever known her. And, of course, what was unutterably poignant and unbearable was that she was clearly insane.

The rain streamed over the window pane. I heard it dripping harshly from some leak in the guttering. And then I heard footsteps in the corridor outside. I felt I could not bear to face Brilliant again, but as the key turned in the lock I knew that I had to face him. The door was flung open, and once more in the dim light of the corridor stood the foreshortened, ridiculous, frightening figure.

He was again disguised as a woman. The melon-hat came down to the pimple of a nose, the fur-collar came up to the large ears, the little elephant legs were concealed. The knife was not, however, hidden. He did not come into the room.

'Powder,' he said, 'I don't know who you are or what your game is. And I don't know what will happen to you when I've gone. But I've one thing to say to you – keep your trap shut. If you ever get the chance to open your trap to anyone about me or what's happened here – don't take it. Keep it shut. It will be better for you.'

He enraged me. His poetry stank and so did he. My temper sent the blood going once again at a decent rate through my veins, and immediately I felt less ill.

'What is going to happen to me?' I said, with false calm.

'I don't know,' he said maliciously. 'I shan't be here to see.'

He stepped forward and took the handle of the door. I could not bear to see him shutting me in and getting away; he was as nonchalant about it as though he were a housewife going off shopping.

Before the door was completely closed, I said: 'I shall open my trap as wide as I can because it is clear to me, Brilliant, that you shot William Preece.'

The door opened again as though it were alive, and Brilliant hurled himself at me and pinned me against the wall. Incredibly I felt the point of his knife against the actual flesh of my stomach. It was the astonishing, fearful second before being stabbed.

'What do you know about Preece?' breathed the dwarf. 'What do you know?'

'Rhoda told me. Rhoda to –'

'How could she, liar?'

'She knows. She told –'

'You said she told you about Bender and De'ath.'

'She told me about them as well. She's ill – mentally ill – '

'I'll kill you if you don't tell me the truth. How did you know about Preece? How did you know?'

The point was trembling. 'Don't,' I said. 'Don't. Don't.' I stopped then. From far below in the house came a dreadful knocking. The dwarf's face – so close that I could count the watch-spring hairs that curled from his cheeks under his slate eyes, trace the tiny red veins above the broad wings of his nose – and, with it, the absurd hat, turned slowly towards the door to listen. The knocking, which, though loud, had been the spaced knocking of someone asking for admittance, changed to the battering noise which accompanies the breaking down of doors. In that moment I wondered, with awful clarity, whether Brilliant would stick me before he ran for it.

But I think he already had forgotten about me. He whirled about for a second like a mouse in an experimental psychologist's maze, and then made a dash for the corridor. I could not prevent him, but I staggered after him. He was not in the corridor. I looked over the banisters down the well of the staircase, but could see no one. The battering noise stopped abruptly and I discerned, far below me in the hall, the bright metal and dark blue of a policeman's helmet, presented in plan. And then another, and another. A loud Yorkshire voice came floating up the well.

'Master French!' it called. 'Master French!' It belonged to the divine Toller. 'The old reliable police,' I said to myself exultingly.

As soon as I had said it my exultation died. There were feverish padding footsteps, and back up the stairs and along the passage towards me toiled Brilliant on his inadequate legs. His skirts were gathered up in one hand, his knife still in the other. The hat had slipped half over his sweaty face. But there was nothing ludicrous about him; he was a terrible and pathetic figure. I never thought once of trying to stop him. Indeed, I pressed myself close against the banister so that I should not impede his way in the slightest degree. I shall never forget how he ran past me, neither of us speaking a word, his eyes staring in front of him.

Without moving my head I could see that he turned at the end of the corridor and went up the next flight of stairs to the second floor. Only then could I bring myself to do anything. I leaned over the banisters and shouted hysterically: 'I'm here. Here. Here.' By the time Toller had come up to me I was, involuntarily but shamefully, weeping. He put his navy-blue overcoated arm round my shoulders, and that made me weep more. 'Nay, lad,' he said, 'it's all over now.' Policemen encircled me.

I swallowed a great piece of emotion and said in a cracked voice: 'He's upstairs. Hurry. He's got a knife.'

'Keep a good eye on him, Arthur,' said Toller, tramping off. To my greater shame I found myself alone with Detective-Constable Jones, who was looking at me curiously and holding out his handkerchief. So as not to seem mean, I took it and dashed out my tears.

I said to Jones: 'Come on. You don't want to miss being in at the death, do you?'

'O.K. It's up to you,' he said, in his abrupt manner.

We went off together up the stairs to the second floor. There was a narrow landing, the dark paper hanging off the walls like unrolled bandages, a fly-spotted light shade, the tarnished brass end of a bed. We found Toller and the policemen crowded in a small back room. There was a strong odour of rain-wet uniforms. A sergeant with a purple face was just climbing courageously on a broken chair to get at a ladder which, hinged at the ceiling end, was intended as a way up to the trap-door in the ceiling at which everyone was gazing. Toller lit a cigarette; its smoke added a new and pungent smell to the room.

When he saw me, Toller said: 'He's up there.'

The sergeant pulled the ladder down and started climbing up it.

'Are you all right, young sir?' asked Toller, watching the sergeant.

'Yes, thank you.' I watched the sergeant, too. His head came to the trap-door. He balanced himself by widening the gap between his feet on the rung and then thrust with the flat of his hands against the trap. His face became a shade more purple, but the trap did not move.

'He's standing on it,' said the sergeant. There was a moment of silence and the sergeant said: 'Bates, come up on the ladder.

Wellman, get on the chair. Bates, you and me will push, while Wellman tries to get his truncheon in.'

The three policemen arranged themselves like acrobats. Sweat began to glisten on the sergeant's face. At last one side of the trap started to lift and the constable called Wellman forced his truncheon in the gap. I could not help imagining Brilliant in the darkness of the underdrawing straining his feet against the terrible pressure.

'Come on, now,' said the sergeant through the gap. 'It won't do you no good staying there. Come out quietly.'

Everyone listened intently, but there was no answer. Wellman was levering cautiously with his truncheon and soon the gap was wide enough for Bates to get his truncheon in, too.

'How did you get my letter?' I asked Toller. I was, for some reason, whispering.

'It came through the post. Got to me this morning,' he said. 'Fourpence to pay on it.'

The sergeant put his hands in the gap and pulled at the trap-door. Bates and Wellman levered strenuously. Suddenly the sergeant gave a grunt, and pulled his hands away. He held them in front of him, as though they did not belong to him, and we saw that they were bleeding. Some drops fell with an unpleasant splash on the dusty floor.

'Whoever said he'd got a knife was a truthful bastard,' said the sergeant, coming down the ladder.

Another policeman took his place and Toller held Wellman round the thighs so that the latter could climb on the chair-back and get a better purchase for his truncheon. The acrobats shifted and strained, and all at once – quite easily, it seemed – the trap-door went slithering away, and revealed a dark gap into the loft. Wellman jumped down from the chair-back and Toller went nimbly up the ladder, passing adroitly the policeman who was already on it. Detective-Constable Jones followed him. Toller disappeared into the loft.

Brilliant's courage must have failed him; he could have stabbed Toller in that instant, but he didn't. There was a brief scuffling over our heads and then a dreadful cry of pain. Immediately after the cry the plaster near the trap collapsed in a great dusty shower, and we saw, projecting through the ceiling, a suède shoe at the end of a short, thick leg. Jones passed into the loft. The leg was pulled back. In a few moments Brilliant was being lowered through the open trap into Wellman's outstretched arms on the ladder. Brilliant's eyes were half-shut, his face was streaked with grime, his lips swollen and bleeding. Wellman and Bates hurried him savagely out of the room; as he passed I think he saw me.

Toller came down from the loft and stood by me, brushing down his overcoat.

'Well, lad,' he said, 'the case is all over bar the shouting.'

'I suppose so,' I said. I felt very tired indeed.

'Thanks to you,' said the Inspector. 'But I'm not going to ask you any questions now. Home and a hot bath and bed for you, lad. And then perhaps tomorrow we'll have a statement from you. You're going to be just about the chief witness, you know.'

We all went downstairs, and Toller ushered me into one of the police-cars, covered me with a rug, and shook hands. There was no sign of Brilliant.

'Sorry I can't come with you,' said Toller. 'But I've a job of work to do with your little friend. Good-bye for now.'

The car drove down the hill into Checklock. There were crowds of people in the streets by the station.

'It's very busy,' I said to the constable who was driving me, making conversation.

'Checklock races today,' he said. 'Know anything for the two-thirty?'

I laughed politely. My tired eyes followed the flicking windscreen wiper for a few moments, and then, of their own volition, closed, and I went into a dead sleep.

*

When I awoke, the first thing I saw was my father's face peering through the car window. The constable was there, too, opening the door.

'What have you been doing?' said my father. 'Murder or arson?'

His car was outside the house as well; evidently he had just come back from the cottage because he still wore the curious tweed hat he always affected in the country. It seemed astonishing that all that had happened with Rhoda and with Brilliant had only taken a week-end.

'I'm innocent,' I said, staggering out of the car. 'And the police,' I said to the constable, 'love me, don't they?'

'He's a blinking hero,' said the constable.

'Goodness!' exclaimed my father. 'Shall I have to hear about it all?'

'Certainly,' I said, 'but not until I'm outside some bacon and eggs. Do you think you could persuade Mrs Mac to bring them to me in bed?'

'If you insist,' said my father.

'Good morning, sir,' said the constable, saluting.

I went in the house in a dream. I fell asleep in the bath, and again over the last slice of toast. When I awoke my room was dark, and my luminous wristwatch said five to eight.

*

For a long time I lay without turning on the light. The curtains moved slightly in the air from the open window; I could hear very faintly that my father was playing *The Magic Flute* records – the strange scene where the three ladies kill the serpent. I turned on my face and wept, with a curious satisfaction, into the pillow. I could not make my thoughts be of anything except the girl, and how far she was from me, and how inane our relationship had been.

In the end I saw that it was no use lying there, and so I switched the light on, got up, and dressed. My room was just as it had been before; the copy of *The Black Dwarf* was still on the bedside table, only now it had no mystery or significance at all for me. When my eyes had stopped looking red I went along to the library, sat in a chair opposite my father, and we listened together to the rest of the first act of the opera. My father pressed the extension switch of the radio-gramophone on the arm of his chair, and the thing shut itself off. We sat in silence for a while, avoiding each other's eyes.

At last I said: 'Toller says I've solved the Preece case.'

'So I gather,' said my father. 'He has been on the telephone wanting to speak to you. I didn't care to rouse you. The second time he telephoned I had a word or two with him.'

'Did he tell you all that had happened?'

'I don't think he knew all that had happened. He said you had been in a tight corner. Have you?'

'I suppose so.' I looked at him; he was looking at his cigar ash. 'I'm sorry, Father.'

'My dear boy, there is nothing to be sorry about. I have had a very restful week-end and I thought you were having one, too. You have not, as you never have, caused me a moment's concern. There is just one thing.' He deposited the two-inch-long cylinder of ash in the ash-tray. 'Let me – or MacBean or someone – know where you're off to on future occasions.' His voice was very apologetic.

'Yes, I will. Only there won't be any future occasions. The case is over.'

'You don't sound very sure about it.'

'That's because I don't understand it.'

'Perhaps Inspector Toller understands it. He left his extension number in case you wanted to ring him.'

'I'll ring him, then. I've got to give him a statement, too. I shall be a witness at Elshie's trial – they caught him, you know.'

'What a degrading beginning to a legal career – a witness at the Old Bailey,' said my father.

'Father,' I said, 'do you mind if I don't tell you all about it, after all.'

'Not in the least, Frederick.'

'I would like to tell you later on, when I've got it all straight.'

'You are going to get it straight?'

'When Toller has got it straight, then. I think I'll telephone him now.'

'On your way out,' said my father, 'perhaps you'll be kind enough to arrange the discs of the second act on the turntable.'

★

I telephoned from the little room on the ground floor which my father used as a study. The green-shaded lamp on the desk threw shadows on the books and the grey walls. I took the telephone, put it on the bookcase, which held the volumes of the *Encyclopaedia Britannica,* and made myself comfortable in the leather-covered easy-chair next to it. For some time I looked at the telephone as though it were a lethal weapon I was about to use on myself. At last I picked it up, without having decided what to tell Toller, and got through to him.

'Frederick French here, Inspector.'

The Yorkshire voice sounded tired. 'I'm glad you rang up. How are you, lad?'

'Absolutely recovered, thank you.'

'I only wanted to tell you that Brilliant's prints match up with those on the revolver. I thought you'd like to know.'

I could only half understand the relief that I felt. 'Then there's no doubt about it?'

'No doubt at all. Brilliant did it.'

I thought for a moment and then I said: 'Do you know why?'

'He won't talk. We've been at him for twelve hours and he won't talk. Now he wants a lawyer.'

'What will you do?'

'We shall charge him with the murder. We don't really care whether he talks or not. There's the fingerprints and we've three witnesses to identify him as the man who ran out of court after the shot had been fired. That's good enough to hang him.'

'Why do you think he did it?'

'It's not our job to show a motive, you know.'

'I suppose not,' I said.

'But our people are down in Heathstead now trying to link Brilliant up with Preece. But, you know, lad, I'm hoping your statement will help us.'

My heart started pounding. Toller went on: 'How did you get on to him?'

I meant my lips to form the words, but they wouldn't. It was no use; Toller would have to find out about Rhoda Savage himself.

'A letter . . .' I said, and then: 'Look, Inspector, it's a very long story.'

'All right, lad, if you're not up to it. I'll be round first thing in the morning. Will nine o'clock be too early?'

'No, of course not.'

Toller started talking again, but I wasn't listening. Before nine o'clock tomorrow morning I had to warn Rhoda of what I was going to tell Toller. More than that; I had to find out how precisely Rhoda had come to know Brilliant; I had to find out about De'ath; I had to find out why the dwarf had shot Preece. In fact, I had to solve the case. It was never so confused and baffled as then. How could I possibly tell Toller the story which Rhoda had told me? And I knew so well what Toller's reaction would be once I divulged that it was Rhoda who – innocently, guiltily, madly, sanely, coincidentally – had put me on to Brilliant; he would, without any hesitation at all, arrest her as an accessory. Technically, whatever her connexion with the case, she *was* an accessory to the murder – that Brilliant was wanted by the police had been in the newspapers and on the radio and she had kept quiet. Except to me. Why was that? Did De'ath really exist? Was the story of the sinister doctor and the handsome secretary true in its essentials even though ludicrously adorned by Rhoda's imagination? If so, how did Preece come to be shot? Preece, the most commonplace, the most normal of all the protagonists of the drama?

This was only a fraction of what went on in my brain as Toller talked. Eventually I became aware that he kept repeating one phrase.

'What's that?' I said.

'The dwarf's mad. He had encephalitis as a child,' he said. 'This is a bad line we're on. I don't seem to be able to make you hear. Yes, Brilliant is mad. That's what we think here. There may be no rational motive at all. Just took a pistol to a public place and loosed it off. There have been such cases before. I remember in Huddersfield in '26 . . .'

He droned away, and my own thoughts started up again. As one does sometimes when one is particularly rapt, my body started acting independently of my mind, and I leaned forward and picked out of the bookcase by me the EDWA to EXTRACT volume of the *Encyclopaedia*. I opened it and began turning over the pages, looking for 'encephalitis'.

'That's how it is, anyway,' concluded Toller. 'I shall be round tomorrow morning.'

'EGYPTOLOGY', I read, and 'ELIXIR'. 'Fine, Inspector,' I said. 'Thank you for everything.'

'Thank *you*, lad,' he said. 'Good-bye.'

'Good-bye,' I said. I put the telephone back on the cradle, still furiously thinking, still automatically turning over the pages, EMIN PASHA, ENIGMA (too far), and (still too far) ENGRAVING.

'In its widest signification' (said the *Encyclopaedia*), 'engraving is the art of cutting lines or furrows on plates, blocks or other shapes of metal, wood, or other material. In this sense the craft has been used for decorative purposes from remote antiquity. In the narrower connotation with which this article is concerned, i.e. engraving for the sake of printing impressions on paper or allied fabrics, the art cannot be traced back before the Christian era. By a transference of terminology,' (went on the *Encyclopaedia*, a trifle tartly), 'illogical but stereotyped by usage, these impressions or prints are also called engravings. In the still more limited signification of line-engraving, the art does not go back before the first half of the fifteenth century.

'The term is used, however, in a looser sense to include all the methods of engraving, cutting, or treating plates, or blocks of metal, wood, or stone, for printing impressions . . .' The article went off into technicalities, but it was with difficulty that I stopped reading it – the words were charged with a vague but incomprehensible significance.

I found myself staring blankly at a page of illustrations of ellipsographs. I must pull myself together, I thought. I turned quickly to the entry I was looking for.

'ENCEPHALITIS LETHARGICA, a disease of the brain characterized by coma (sleepy sickness). The virus is unknown . . .' I skipped over symptoms and something called 'The Parkinsonian Syndrome', which looked interesting, and got to a paragraph headed 'Mental Changes'. 'These,' it said, 'are of great importance from their frequency and character and are present to some extent in about 75 per cent of cases. The changes may be of all grades, from slight weakness of the intellectual powers to definite dementia and insanity . . . some irritability of temper . . .

insomnia ... definite alterations in the moral character ...'

When I had finished reading it Brilliant's personality and life were fixed firmly and clearly for me by the inescapable physical facts of the disease. I pitied him and understood him. If only one could be sure that he would keep silence, it would be best perhaps for him to take all the responsibility for the murder and end his days safely locked up as a criminal lunatic.

I paced in and out of the circle of light thrown by the lamp on the carpet and then sat down at the desk to write a letter.

Dear Father (I wrote),

If you find that I have gone, this is to say that I haven't gone without considering it very seriously, and also to let you know where I've gone. I simply have to go to –

When I had written this there was a knock at the door and I covered up the letter with some blotting paper and said: 'Come in.' It was Mrs MacBean with a tray.

'Your father said I was to bring you some supper, Master Frederick,' she said.

'Oh, Mrs Mac,' I said with false good humour, 'that's very good of you.'

'It's nothing but the pigeon-pie you missed at dinner – cold.'

'Delicious.'

She put the tray on the desk and stood for a moment pulling at the hairs which grew, like the withered stalk on plucked tomatoes, from the sides of her mouth.

'Did you sleep till now?'

'Yes,' I said.

'Ach, the dear,' she wailed disapprovingly. 'Whatever had you been up to?'

'Murder most foul, as in the best it is.'

She turned in a baffled way and waddled off. She delivered a parting shot at the door: 'Dinna eat too much of the pie.'

The pie was sticking in my gullet – and yet I was hungry. A sense of the shortness of time beat urgently at the pit of my stomach. And then I saw on the tray for the first time what had been facing me since Mrs MacBean had come in. It stood there next to the butter dish and the Camembert cheese – a tin of Abernethy biscuits. It changed, in my visionary stare, into the tallness of Mr Brown and became pink and fringed with white hair. It was like putting the right key out of a bunch of keys into an obstinate lock. I stood up excitedly, screwed up the letter to my father, and dashed out of the house.

*

In the train, empty at that between-time hour of the evening, I thought ridiculously that when I spoke to Rhoda I would bring myself to use her Christian name. I gazed out of the window over the dark viaduct on which, like gold bracelets, other trains were running, over the London roofs, and thought how the train was remorselessly eating up the miles between us. I looked forward to being with her as one looks forward to the rich companionship of an absorbing novel. I should warn her of Brilliant's capture and she would tell me that she was in no danger, that she was not involved, and we would arrange to meet again. Or she would say that she had not been able to avoid being involved, and I would then hide her until the affair blew over, visiting her in her captivity. Once again I tried to imagine her face and could not: should I recognize her when I saw her?

When I came out of the station at Heathstead, a fine rain started to fall, and I realized that I had brought no coat. An old man with an old dog on a lead turned into the Railway Arms. Another man came past on a bicycle. A white cat padded across the road; the unlighted shop windows had a melancholy look. I turned my collar up and set out towards the heath.

It was very deserted. The lamps and the trees were reflected in the black pond, their images pricked by the rain. I seemed to be walking into an uninhabited and sinister country, and suddenly I was frightened. Rhoda was such a small person to find among these thousands of houses. And here was all the intrigue, all the desires and hatreds which had boiled over and killed Preece. At this moment I nearly turned back to telephone Toller and tell him everything. And then I thought of the police bursting into Savage's house and finding Rhoda and her father reading

Mrs Gaskell by the fire. So I went on, becoming more and more dubious, more and more convinced that Toller was right, that all the hints which I had had during the case and had now added up into a shadowy but monstrous paraphernalia of plot were figments only of my own imagination. Anyway, so far as the actual murder was concerned, who but the dwarf could have done it? There remained the problem of how to keep Rhoda out of it. What could I tell Toller? That I had found a letter written by Brilliant from the Checklock address? But to whom and where?

Meanwhile I approached nearer and nearer to Wren Road.

*

It was very dark, and the lamps in these quiet streets were spaced at long intervals. It was this and my absorbing thoughts which made me miss my way and at last find myself (as I recognized) at the entrance to a mews overhung by trees, which ran at the back of Wren Road. Because Number 2 was the first house, it was easy to distinguish – or, rather, its back gate was: the house itself was hidden in the gloom at the other end of what must have been, judging by the distance I had come, a long garden. I ploughed through the mud and puddles and came up to the gate. Behind it loomed a low building, which I took to be a former stable. I stood for a moment, hearing the dripping of the rain from the trees, and then pressed down the latch of the gate and pushed. It opened with a slight groan, and I stepped into the garden. The rain formed transparent, faintly glistening curtains against the velvet darkness. To my right lay the stable buildings: the path I went along led me to them. Their large double doors were open a little. In the gap they made I saw – when it was much too late to hide or to draw back – that someone was standing, muffled, motionless, and silent.

I turned to cold stone. The figure there must have seen me, but it still did not speak or move. Instead, as I could see from a red glow that blossomed like the striking of a neon tube, it took a pull at a cigarette. Since there was nothing else for it, I walked forward.

When I had taken a few steps the figure said, in a voice whose tones – to me strange and touching – I had forgotten but which were at once beautifully familiar: 'Hello, Frederick. I knew you'd come.'

'Rhoda,' I said, as I had imagined. When I got up to her I saw that she had a raincoat draped over her head and shoulders.

'Were you waiting for me?' I said.

'Yes.'

'But how did you know?'

'I knew.' Her cigarette end made a red arc as she threw it away.

'We are in a dreadful mess. They've caught Brilliant.'

'I know.'

'How did you know?'

'Oh, never mind that, Frederick. We haven't time. Did you tell them about me?'

'Of course not. That's why I've come. I shall have to tell them.'

'Why?'

'What else can I tell them?'

'You mustn't tell them.'

'But you've nothing to do with it, have you?'

'Of course I haven't, Frederick; of course I haven't.'

'Why did you tell me those lies about Brilliant – and De'ath and the rest?' I was breathless. 'Why did you?'

'You wouldn't have believed the truth.'

'What is the truth?'

'Don't cross-examine me. I won't hear it. I said you needn't help me. Everyone is against me.'

She seemed very child-like as she said this. It was so dark; if I could have seen her face it would have helped. As it was, I seemed to be talking into emptiness.

'Listen,' I said. 'Brilliant killed Preece. The police are going to charge him with it. I shall have to tell them how I found him.'

'How did you get the police to Checklock? Did you take them with you?'

'No, no. I believed you until I saw Brilliant and the house. I believed you.'

'You mustn't tell the police about me.'

'Then what is the truth? Do you know why Brilliant did the murder? How did you know where he was hiding? Don't you see that I shall have to know the truth if I'm going to concoct a story for the police?'

She came closer, and I felt her breath, warm and laden with the smell of cigarette smoke, on my face.

I said: 'This is murder. I've got to be sure that Brilliant did it. And then I don't mind telling as many lies as you like – for you. But there is so little time.'

'Frederick,' she whispered, 'you can put them off quite easily. Say you found a letter with Elshie's address on it.'

'A letter!' I exclaimed, stupidly.

'Yes.'

'But where did I find it?'

'It dropped out of Mrs Preece's bag.'

'Mrs Preece! What has she got to do with it?'

'Everything,' said Rhoda Savage.

*

I was sweating like a pig. I took out my handkerchief and wiped my face. Rain was running from the roof of the stable building and dripping noisily into the gravel by our feet.

I said: 'It won't do. You've got to tell me the whole story. I can't bring Mrs Preece into it unless I'm certain that she's involved. If I tell the police I got to Brilliant through her they'll arrest her at once.'

'Don't you think it's better that they should arrest her rather than me?'

'Yes. Yes, I do. But, Rhoda, what are you holding back from me? We can't go on like this.'

'Do the police know you've come here?'

'Of course they don't. I've come to keep you out of it. What is this about Mrs Preece?'

She sighed very deeply. She took hold of my arm above the elbow. 'I'll tell you everything,' she said.

'It's the only way. I've guessed a lot.'

Her fingers tightened. 'What?'

'That you wanted Brilliant to get hold of me. So you told me the story about De'ath. De'ath doesn't exist.'

She laughed rather shrilly. 'De'ath doesn't exist – are you a spiritualist?'

'What do you know about the spiritualists?'

'What do you mean?'

'Nothing. Nothing. Oh, Rhoda!'

'Go on; you were telling me what you'd guessed.'

'You said you'd tell me the truth. We're going round in circles. We've hardly any time. You'll have to hide until the case is all over.'

'What else did you guess?'

'The person you are protecting.' She released my arm, and I felt that she was slipping away from me altogether. There was a long silence, at the back of which the rain streaming from the stable roof roared like the sound track of a talking film. A profound sadness overtook me as I realized once more her elusive nature and the vagueness of our friendship.

She said at last in a subdued voice: 'Yes, I'll tell you everything.'

'It's about time.' It was a relief to be exasperated with her.

'We can't talk here, though. There is so much to tell, Frederick. Come into the house.'

'But what about your father?'

'He isn't there tonight. There's no one there.' She took hold of my arm again and led me along the path towards the house.

'Will you still come to see me when it's all over,' she was saying.

My exasperation dissolved. 'Yes,' I said.

The garden was a jungle. We dodged through trees, and brambles tore at us; the path degenerated into long grass. And then, emerging from the bushes, I saw before us the house. Chinks of light from windows in the basement came to us, lighting up some of the rods of rain. I stopped dead.

'You said your father wasn't in.'

She said, reassuringly: 'I left the lights on when I came out.'

And then, from the direction of the house, setting all the pulses in my body going madly, came a bass voice.

'Is that you, Pussy?'

I tried to see her face. But it was lost in the darkness.

'Pussy?' growled the voice.

'Yes, Ben,' called Rhoda, lightly and easily as though she were trying to put me at ease. 'Pussy here.'

I turned and ran back wildly into the bushes. I heard her call my name, but I paid no attention. And then sensed her at my heels. Her little lemur's claws caught at my arm and shoulder. I tried to shake her off, but she could run like a stag. Branches whipped stingingly across my face. Long before we reached the stable-building I felt myself falling and had to stop. I turned to deal with her, but she seized my outstretched hand in a delicate grip, pulled me towards her and by dint of at once stopping and turning – so that her shoulder acted as fulcrum and my arm as lever – she threw me in one agile movement over her head and on to my back. I lay on the wet grass, gazing stupefiedly at the black sky, feeling the rain speckling my face. But she did not let me lie comfortably there. She hauled me up, my left wrist in her left hand, twisted my arm a little, and, pressing gently above my elbow with her other, led me back through the bushes. It was astonishing and shameful. I waved my right arm in the air ineffectually, tried in vain to straighten my stooped body; when I made my steps reluctant she simply pressed a little harder with her right hand, and I went with her like a child.

'You ought to take ju-jitsu lessons,' she remarked.

'Perhaps sometime you'll give me them,' I managed to say.

'I was taught by a friend of Elshie's, called Tokio Smith. He has a gymnasium in Soho.'

She chatted heartlessly until we came to the house. A man walked up the basement steps, and said: 'What's going on, Pussy? The boss'll kill you for this.'

'It's the judge's son – the boy I told you about, Ben. Only you didn't believe me.'

'You are such a flaming liar, Pussy.'

'I put him off before, but I couldn't put him off again.'

'I don't know what you're talking about, Pussy. I'm flamed if I do. What are we going to do with him?'

'I don't know. That's up to you.'

'Not me,' said Ben. 'You're a flaming nuisance, Pussy. Don't you think we've got enough to do?'

'Should I have let him go to the police then?'

'What would he want to go to the police for?'

'Oh, Ben, you are dumb.'

'I know I'm dumb. I don't bring schoolboys along at a time like this. Listen, Pussy, are the garage doors open?'

'Yes. Ben, where shall I put him?'

I could only see in the light from the basement this man's trousers owing to my bowed attitude. They were well filled with fat legs.

'Now he's here,' said Ben in his slow, obtuse voice, 'he'll have to go in the cellars. You sure the doors are open? We're ready to move some of the things.'

'Sure, Ben.'

Ben's legs passed out of my orbit. 'Come on,' said Rhoda, propelling me down the basement steps. She gave me a final push into a lighted room. As I straightened up I saw her lock the door and put the key in the pocket of the cyclamen-coloured corduroy trousers she was wearing. We gazed at each other like boxers introduced in the ring. Her hair was not, as it had been before, arranged on top of her head, but loose on her shoulders. I saw finally, out of all the shapes she had assumed in reality and in my imagination, that she was no older than I was. What had perverted the intelligence and energy that she showed in all her movements and speech?

'Well, Pussy?' I said. I felt a good deal better now I was out of her bewildering grasp.

'I don't like that name,' she said.

'Are you still going to tell me what it's all about?' I said.

'I think we can skip that nonsense.' She put both hands in her pockets and looked at the floor.

'It was all nonsense, then?' I knew that I was still trying to save something out of the wreck.

'Yes.'

'I didn't think it was.'

She shrugged her shoulders.

'Rhoda,' I said. 'It's not too late. Unlock the door, and come with me to the police. Please. Please come.'

'Don't be a fool.'

'It's murder. A man was shot. I saw him die on the floor. Nothing can justify that.'

'You don't understand anything,' she said.

'You needn't betray anybody. I'm not asking you to do that. Only please get away from –'

'Oh, shut up.' She walked to an oil-stove standing in the middle of the room. There was a teapot on it. On the floor nearby was a plate with a pale, revolting, speckled seed cake on it. 'Do you want a cup of tea?' she said.

I shook my head. She poured herself a black one into a pint mug, adding a spoonful of condensed milk out of a tin, and sat down, to sip it, on a packing-case. The room was small; torn paper littered the floor; there were oil-drums in one corner and a bench with a vice and other tools. It looked not like a room in a house but a room in a factory. There was another door besides the one at which we had come in. I sidled towards it. Rhoda's little animal's face was hidden in the mug. I made a leap for the door-handle, seized it, turned it, and pulled.

'That's locked, too,' Rhoda said. It was. I leaned my back against it, and said, with an air of nonchalance that I hoped did not look too false. 'Well, what's going to happen to me?'

'Don't be in such a hurry. I haven't finished my tea.'

'And then?'

'The boss will say.'

It was grotesque, but it was true. This girl incongruously mixed up in what was going on in the house – like a child who serves amateurly in the family shop; the ridiculous but commonplace way in which both she and Ben referred to the concealed and mysterious 'boss'; the casual circumstances which surrounded my capture. It seemed to me then that if I only exerted my will I could escape easily enough; or at least smash down the fantasy of conspiracy and crime (that might well have been spun merely from Rhoda's head) and reveal the normal truth behind it. Yes, it was like that, only Rhoda and Ben were real and living, just as Brilliant had been real and living, with the monstrous characters of more ordinary people – to which their abnormal activities seemed attached as transitorily and trivially as a bright ticket to an old familiar hat in a cloakroom.

There came a banging on the outside door. For a second my heart exulted; a thought that once more Toller had somehow found out where I was, and come, like the hero of a Western, to rescue me. Rhoda put her mug cautiously on the ground. And then Ben's voice boomed through the door.

'Open up, Pussy,' he said.

She fished the key out and unlocked the door. Ben came in, blinking in the light. His body was as fat as his legs, and he wore a cloth cap.

'What's the matter?' asked Rhoda.

It was dream-like, unbelievable, but I knew Ben's face as well as I knew my father's clerk's.

'Don't be so flaming jumpy, Pussy,' he said. 'Everything's going to be all right.'

But I simply could not remember where I had seen him before. His face was as instantaneously unplaceable as the face of a shop assistant one sees away from the shop.

He said: 'Have you supped all the tea, Pussy?'

'There's some in the pot,' said Rhoda. 'Is that what you made all the banging for?'

I was even thinking of places I went into when I was at school; the bookshop, the soda-fountain, the sports-outfitters.

Ben sat down on the packing-case. 'Pour me a cup, Puss.'

Rhoda took up the teapot and the flower of light from the top of the oil-stove appeared on the ceiling. She passed Ben the mug. He had cut himself a piece of cake, whose arc subtended a very obtuse angle indeed, and was eating it like a lion. 'Can't abide seed cake,' he said, with his mouth full. 'Can't abide it.' He crammed the last lump into his mouth and chewed rudely and with apparent relish.

'It's going to take some shifting,' he went on, 'the what-do-you-call it.' He put a cigarette in his mouth; against his big face it looked like a tooth-pick. I stared at him, as a snake is said to stare at a fakir, until he grew slightly blurred, but still I could not place him. And then, when he had lit his cigarette and taken up the mug from the floor, with a comfortable gesture he eased his cap from his forehead to the back of his head, and I saw, protruding from the greasy grey strands of his hair, an enormous yellow wen. Doors opened successively along the passage of my mind. I saw the brilliant green of Westsea Racecourse, the crowds, the shouting, the coloured horses – and Ben, who systematically backed all the horses in the race with new five-pound notes.

'I've got to take the boy along to see him,' Ben was saying. 'You're in for it, Pussy. He's as mad as a fly in a bottle.'

Once again the excitement of the case, the horror and the intrigue of the puzzle, took hold of me; a lump appeared in my gullet; my hands were trembling so much that I had to hide them in my pockets. I no longer wanted Toller to come and rescue me, or to escape with Rhoda. All I wanted was to know precisely and in detail what Preece's murder had been about. I wanted to see those mysterious creatures who, as well as Rhoda and Ben, were in this house. For whether Brilliant had done the actual killing or not, it was clear that he was merely a cog in the machinery of which I had had a glimpse – the machinery of Ben, of the lorry in the stable building, and, finally, of this house. For, I saw clearly, it was because of the house that Preece had been killed – why had I not realized it long ago? The case in my father's court had been about nothing else. And it was to keep me away from the house that Rhoda had invented De'ath. And now, now that Brilliant had been captured and the case was beginning to gape open, it was the house that was being abandoned.

'I've got to take the boy along to see him.' Here it was then – the classic revelation of the identity of the mastermind.

Ben was still rambling on – his words reverberated from the depths of the pint mug. 'Did you open the garage doors, Pussy?' He had a one-track mind. He finished his tea at last, and stood up, pulling his cap over his forehead again.

'Come on,' he said to me. It was the first time he had looked at me since he came in. I knew his face so well that I could hardly believe that he didn't know mine; instinctively I averted it from him.

Rhoda said: 'I'll come, too.'

'Nix,' said Ben. 'You're out of this, Puss. You've done enough flaming damage.'

'But I want to know what's going to happen to him.'

I glanced at her, but she was standing at the bench, turning the handle of the vice, her head bent, her hair over her cheek, hiding her eye. I wanted more than anything to see the look on her face. Already I had forgotten the chase through the garden and the cruelty of her words afterwards. I only remembered her sharp hands and her blue eyes.

'I'll tell you what happens,' said Ben, strolling over to me and taking hold of my wrist. She did not say anything else and neither did I, but when Ben had unlocked and taken me through the inner door, and I was standing in a dark passage while with one hand he clumsily relocked it, I knew that I should have spoken, that I should always regret not having spoken. I felt that I had lost any chance I had of ever being happy again.

When Ben straightened up, although I could not properly see him, I sensed a dreadful change in his attitude towards me. It was as though he had abandoned the self that drank tea, and said Puss, in the room we had just left; what remained was the fat body, the stupid face, and the mind that had made him a part of the case. He walked along the passage, still grasping my wrist, but as though I was not with him. At the end of the passage we went through a door which led directly to a flight of stone steps down to the cellars. Ben switched on a light. On the way down we passed shelves with household things on them – a meat-hook, a dish-cover, a jar labelled 'Damson – 2nd boiling' in feminine handwriting. For some reason these things seemed very sinister. When we got to the bottom I could hear someone moving about, and the occasional clank of metal on metal.

A man's voice echoed round the whitewashed walls: 'Where the hell have you been, Ben?'

Ben did not reply to this. He called: 'I've got the boy here. Shall I bring him in?'

The voice swore again; it was very bad-tempered. 'No. Take him in the store.'

Ben led me into the store. It was a small room, with metal shelving on one wall, and some drums of oil on the floor. The shelving was empty except for some torn paper; scraps of paper stained with black ink littered the floor. There was a table and a chair. A naked electric lamp hung from the ceiling. Ben sat in the chair between me and the door. I watched the opening as one watches the perspective of a street waiting for a procession. The scratch of a match with which Ben lit a cigarette sounded like a beam breaking.

The man who came so quietly and so suddenly in at the door that I jumped was as strange to me as someone else's bathroom. He said to Ben: 'It's ready for moving.' He held a heavy spanner in his hand and did not look at me.

Ben said: 'I'll have a dekko.' He went out.

The man laid the spanner on the table and wiped his hands together. He said: 'What has my daughter told you?'

It was Savage, of course. Gradually the faint memory I had of him in court revived. The pattern was proving to be quite regular. I gained a little time by looking nervous and frightened; that did not require much acting. He asked the question again; he seemed only able to speak evenly at all by exercising a kind of obvious control. He was a slim man; his hair was brushed sleekly to his head – it was, though he couldn't have been less than fifty, brown, but a dull, lifeless brown that made it seem false. His face – or, rather, his cheeks and the lower part of his brow – had a glazed flush which was not of health. There were bags under his eyes which seemed to have hard edges. His eyes were as blue as Rhoda's, and glittered with moisture.

'She told me a rigmarole which led me to Brilliant. Nothing else.'

He lit a cigarette from the stub of the one he was smoking. He said: 'What did Brilliant tell you?'

'Nothing. Except about his poetry.'

'What have you found out yourself?'

'What about?' I let my mouth stay open a little in what I hoped was a stupid but not imbecile way.

'What goes on here?'

'I don't know what's going on here. What do you mean, sir?'

His attention constantly wandered: when he recalled it he became immediately irritable.

'We were all friends here of Mr Brilliant,' he said in his quick way. 'We're very concerned about him. He's not responsible for his actions, of course. Liable to do anything. Were you there when the police took him?'

I said I was.

'What did he say?' asked Savage.

'He didn't say anything. As a matter of fact he couldn't – he'd been knocked about a bit. But the Inspector who looks after the case told me tonight that Mr Brilliant wouldn't tell them anything.'

'When did you see the Inspector?'

'I telephoned him.'

'I expect you said you were coming to see Rhoda.'

'Why, sir?'

Savage flicked his ash about ten times with the forefinger of the hand holding his cigarette. 'Your father doesn't object to your seeing my little girl?'

I couldn't, on the spur of the moment, decide whether or not to tell him that I'd come here without anyone's knowledge. I shook my head, but he naturally wasn't satisfied with that.

'Did you tell him you were coming here tonight?'

I compromised: 'No, but he might have guessed.'

He rubbed his eyes and flicked again. 'You'll have to stay here,' he said abruptly. And without more ado he picked his spanner up from the table, walked out, and locked the door of the store behind him.

I sat down in the chair to relieve my aching legs. I had a ridiculous feeling that someone might be watching me through the keyhole, so I threw my arm nonchalantly, but a trifle theatrically, over the chair back, and pursed my lips in a soundless whistle. Savage had, with his negative manner, alarmed me much more than Ben or even Brilliant had. Sitting in this little cellar in the harsh light, I realized, it seemed for the first time, that I knew more than anyone about Preece's murder, and that Savage dare not let me go. Perhaps I should merely stay locked in this place until they had made their getaway with the machinery and whatnot, and until Toller had got round to coming to Wren Road with a search warrant. Perhaps that was too facile a view: perhaps Savage would take me with them. My thoughts raced absurdly on: I imagined myself sitting next to Rhoda in the cab of the lorry, hurtling through the night towards a life of love and crime.

I pulled myself together and looked at my watch. It was precisely midnight.

7   TUESDAY, 11 *September*

AFTER I had tried the door and searched all round the store, I went back to the chair. I must, for a few minutes, have dozed, for when I heard my name being whispered my head was resting on my bent arms on the table and I did not remember putting it there.

'Frederick, Frederick,' came through the keyhole.

I was against the door immediately. 'Rhoda,' I said.

She said: 'I'm sorry, Frederick. Will you forgive me? Will you forgive me?'

My cheek was against the chill, damp wood: I could hear the noise of her breathing. At last her voice had natural and simple tones, and to me it was infinitely pathetic. The melodramatic Rhoda with her hair piled up and her Stevensonesque narrative, the tough Rhoda with her loose hair and clipped speech – both these had vanished.

'Yes,' I said. 'Of course.'

The touching voice came again: 'Can you? Can you really?'

'Yes. Yes.'

'I'm truly sorry for everything.'

'Rhoda, can you get me out?'

This seemed not to have occurred to her. 'Yes,' she said, in a rather surprised way. I heard the key turn in the lock, the door opened, and there she was standing, her hands poised as though she was holding something tiny and fragile.

She said immediately: 'I'm frightened.'

'Of whom?'

'Of what they might do to you.'

'Rhoda, I must get away.'

'Yes.'

'Where are they?'

'In the garage.'

'Can I get through the house and out at the front?'

'I don't know.' Her wits were wandering. 'Yes. Yes, you can.'

'Come on, then. Please, Rhoda.'

'Oh,' she said. 'Oh.'

I looked down the bleak perspective of white, damp-stained walls. It was only by the most crucial of miracles that the fat and the thin figures of my captors did not appear at the end of it. A long cobweb swayed from the ceiling as though it were announcing them. Rhoda had not moved.

I said, with sudden fright: 'What is going to happen to you?'

We stood without speaking for several long seconds. And then she shut the store-room door, locked it, caught my hand, and we flew along the passage. At the head of the cellar steps we shrank against the jam jars while we peered through an inch-wide chink of the door.

'You must come with me,' I breathed.

She shook her head. We emerged into the empty, dark corridor. Along it, in the opposite direction to the workshop, we silently and tediously groped our way. My hand came to the knob of a door. Before I opened it, I whispered: 'You can't stay here, now.'

'I can't come with you,' she said, in a small, stubborn voice. 'How can I come with you? This is my home.'

All the time I was expecting the other door, the workshop door, to open: I couldn't bring myself to utter another word. I turned the knob in my hand as though I was making a decision that would change my whole life. I pushed upon the door, stretched out, and encountered a row of waistcoat buttons.

Ben's voice said: 'What the flaming –' I banged the door before I could hear any more and set off frantically, stumbling down the passage. The light from an electric torch leapt from behind me and threw my shadow grotesquely against the workshop door. Rhoda seemed to have vanished. Ben's arm caught me round the neck. I struggled violently, but without heart: I knew that it was all over.

'How did you get out, you little bastard?' Ben kept saying, with more emotion in his voice than I had ever heard in it before. He hauled me back the way he had come, that is, into the house proper. I caught a glimpse of worn linoleum, a pair of great horns coming from the wall, a bowler hat on one of them, a coloured picture of some eastern temple, and then Ben pushed me into a room.

In the room, standing at a table with his back to me, was a man who was not Savage. At the noise of my entrance the man started and then crouched, covering with his arms what was on the table. That was only a momentary reaction; a second later he had straightened up.

Behind me, Ben said: 'He's got out. I found him in the house. We'll have to do something better with him. He's as –'

The figure at the table turned slowly, and said, in a voice which was frightening in its iciness and contempt: 'You empty-headed, bungling fool, you. What have you brought him in here for?'

'Well, he's got out,' Ben said, 'as you can see.'

'Fool! Fool! Fool!' said the figure at the table. He turned his back on us again, and started putting the pile of clean five-pound notes from the table into a Gladstone bag. He said: 'Now he knows everything. Think about that, will you?'

'Well, he was out,' said Ben, as stupidly as a rebuked schoolboy. 'Something had to be done.'

It was I, not Ben, who was thinking. I knew everything, as I believe I had instinctively known all the time. The last piece of the puzzle fitted neatly into the place where one had always known it must go. The figure at the table was Kekewich.

*

I had forgotten how strange his head was. Against the crimson curtains behind the table his face had an almost violet pallor; the long, ashen, lion's hair disappeared curiously at the back into his coat collar. The nostrils of his emperor's nose had a rawish look.

He said: 'Tie the boy up.'

'I shall have to find some rope,' said Ben. 'But there's a length downstairs I think I can lay my hands on.'

'Get it,' said Kekewich, 'and ask Savage if he's ready for us to help him move.'

'Keep an eye on the boy. He's a slippery little beggar. I just found him in the house.'

'Hurry. Hurry,' said Kekewich.

When Ben had gone, Kekewich closed the bag and came over to me.

'It is a ridiculous situation, isn't it?' he said.

'Yes.'

'That a little girl with too much imagination and some misplaced ingenuity might spoil five years' planning and work, or, to go deeper into causes, that a boy with too much inquisitiveness...'

I can give only a very pale idea of the way he looked at me as he spoke. Although we had met merely for a minute he stared as though he knew me utterly and despised me: he stared fixedly, his head on one side like a great macaw's, with an expression on his face not of amusement, nor curiosity, nor mockery, but something of all three.

'It is ridiculous, isn't it?' he repeated.

The way I had again to say yes – stupidly, weakly, childishly – was only evidence of a trifle of his power. He frightened me. Like Brilliant, there seemed nothing in his character with which I could make contact, which I had in common with him; but, unlike Brilliant, he was intelligent.

He said: 'I think you are the only person who understands everything. Do you agree?'

I had to swallow several times before I could speak. 'The police will understand almost everything soon.'

'Oh, do you think so? Why?'

'I think Brilliant will tell them.'

'You are a very clever boy. You don't like being the only person who understands everything, do you?'

'No.'

'Especially since you are here and no one but us knows you are here.' With very precise movements he lit a cigarette and then held it in the very centre of his tiny mouth. 'What did you think of all the money?'

'I thought Mr Savage had made it very well.'

He took out the cigarette and smiled. 'Such a spirited boy!'

He turned and, seeming to forget my existence, fell to pacing the room. It was a strange sensation to be in that room with its crimson curtains and wallpaper, its shelf of books by the fireplace, the old sofa with wooden arms – the same room which Rhoda had long ago described to me. But it was the setting, not for the far-fetched plot of the young girl and the match-making father which she had persuaded me into accepting, but for the more far-fetched plot of murder and counterfeiting, harder still to accept. For several minutes I stood and he silently walked; I could hear, through the outside wall, rain falling from a leaking gutter with the sound of subdued machine-gun fire. I thought of my father, quietly asleep in Chelsea, never having missed me; of Toller slapping Brilliant's face under an arc-light; of Rhoda sitting alone by the oil-stove in the workshop, her hair over her face.

Ben came back carrying what looked to be a clothesline. For some reason he had discarded his cap: his wen, nestling in his grey, greasy hair, looked like a little present tied carefully with string. He went over to Kekewich on the other side of the table and spoke to him in a low voice. They were too far away for me to hear all the dialogue, but I heard Ben say: 'Can't be done,' and, a little later, Kekewich: '... if it will burn,' and, from this and an occasional other word, I believed that I knew what had happened and what they intended to do. An intense feeling of sickness crept from my stomach to my chest and throat. By comparison, all that I had experienced since the firing of the shot almost a week ago seemed tame and without reality; it was this for which events had been accumulating and arranging themselves, this thing which inexorably was going to happen to me. Part of their machinery, or apparatus, or whatever, could not be removed, and so they intended to destroy it – and other traces of their activities – by burning down the house. And even more than the machinery, they desired to destroy my knowledge. I do not know, and never shall, whether this is what they purposed. When Ben and Kekewich broke off their conversation, and Ben turned away and came padding and waddling over to me, disentangling the rope as absently as though he were about to make up a parcel, I was caught by an uncontrollable terror. All through the case I had been helped by being young, by being, as one always is until one is completely adult, continually underestimated. So it was now: although, if I had thought about it, I should have realized that I could not hope to escape from the three counterfeiters nor even to evade them for more than a few minutes. I was sufficiently unguarded to be able to throw myself on the door, wrench it open, and sprawl into the corridor, slamming the door tight behind me.

In the half-second I looked wildly about that dimly-lit hall I saw everything in it as though it had been under a microscope. A hanging coat, a red-leather chair with a high, carved back, a broken-down console table in gilt plaster and marble, a Gothic window embrasure – as hiding places I weighed and rejected them as my eyes flickered over them. In almost the same movement as that in which I had recovered from my sprawl I flattened myself in a doorway next to the one out of which I had just come. It was ridiculous, and yet no sooner had I managed to put some sort of control on my sobbing-like breathing when I saw Ben go lumbering past me, still holding the rope, and shouting for Savage. He disappeared through the door which led to the cellars. There was a terrible silence. A little breeze found its way from the street and gently rippled the rush mat that covered the floor of the hall. And then, in the distance, from the back garden it must have been, but very clear, came three blasts on a police whistle.

*

Believing and yet unbelieving, a relieved happiness about to break through the agitated curtain of my nerves, I took a step forward from my doorway, swallowed, checked my breath with an effort, and painfully listened. The silence fell again. I turned my head and saw, standing stock-still, not a foot from me, a smile on his Nero's face, Kekewich. I started, and felt the blood drain from my face. We looked at each other for what seemed an eternity: I could see, even in the bad light, darkish places on his skin, where patchily, his beard was beginning to grow. The smile was fixed.

A heavy knocking on the front door – which clearly lay through a porch off the hall – brought the awful staring to an end. The knocking, like the knocking which had preceded Brilliant's capture, was obviously designed to break down the door. I seemed to have experienced everything before.

For a few seconds Kekewich did not stir. And then, moving sluggishly, as though he were very tired, he took a step forward, raised his small white hand, and slapped me hard on each cheek. Then he walked slowly to the antlers on the wall, took down the bowler hat which hung there, crammed it on his head, and went through the door which led to the cellars.

I watched him in a trance, my face numb at first, and and then burning. The knocking went on as though it were in my head. And then I felt a huge anger; my teeth ground together like an animal's: I wanted to leap on Kekewich and tear at him. I flung myself after him through the door, along the passage, and down the cellar steps. From halfway down the steps I saw one of the doors in the cellar closing. A few moments later I recklessly opened it, and went headlong over a pile of coal. The only light came from outside the room. In the ceiling I heard a metallic sound. I scrambled up the coal and, reaching out with swaying hands, encountered the perforated, circular, iron grating which covered the aperture through which coal was poured into the cellar. I pushed away the grating, grasped the side of the aperture and, my feet sliding and trampling on the coal, managed to haul myself up and out into the strangely cool and infinite air of the garden.

I knew precisely where I was – in the passage along the side of the house where I had first encountered Rhoda. I knew, too, where Kekewich had gone. Among the trees on the far side of the garden wall was a subdued trampling. There were no policemen, though from far away – the stable-building, I guessed – there came some faint shouting.

I tore a nail almost to the root getting over the wall. I was desperate. The fool Toller, concentrating apparently on the obvious apparatus of escape, was perhaps netting the tiddlers, but Moby Dick was escaping him in the easiest and most casual of ways. And so I ploughed across two gardens after Kekewich. Eventually, I think he must have known that I was following, but, of course, he dared not stop to deal with me so near the police. Perhaps I should have shouted for help, but then, among the bushes and the stone dwarfs and rabbits, the rose-beds and the fruit trees, I hoped still that he was unaware of my pursuit. The rain had stopped, but the gardens were still sopping and smelt grave-like.

*

Several times I thought I had lost him. Until we had got out of the gardens it was always touch and go. But at last, in a narrow alleyway at right-angles to Wren Road, I had a clear view, in the light of a sickly half-moon low in the sky, of his hurrying, grotesquely bowler-hatted figure far ahead. I ran close against the boarded fence, in the shadow, but I do not think I cared very much whether he saw me or not. We were going towards the centre of Heathstead; soon, in spite of the lateness of the hour, I should encounter other people and raise a hue and cry; if I could manage to keep Kekewich in sight he was bound eventually to be captured.

We came out of the alley into a road and then branched into another road. But where Kekewich might have turned on to the heath he kept straight on. The streets began to slope downwards. He was making for the river. It was then that I first thought that he might escape. Under the dark trees, along the wet paving, my eyes on the tripping man away in front, thought after thought, speculation and memory, went through my brain with the speed and freedom of a dream. I thought of Elshie saying: 'They'll get me away tomorrow,' and his large, strongly-coloured papier-mâché face; of the lorry; of a boat on the river which would take them all a thousand miles.

The pace Kekewich was setting at first forced me sometimes from a fast walk to a run, but when we had been going for about a quarter of an hour I found I had no need to run. It occurred to me with surprise that I could almost certainly catch up with him – that in one thing at least, physical condition, I was his superior. I began to feel confident. It was astonishing how, in that chase, there was time for shades of emotion to succeed one another, as though one were lying thinking in bed.

I believe that we went very near the place where the inquest had been held. The streets became meaner. Once when Kekewich stopped and I did likewise I heard, against the distant groaning of an all-night tram, a faint, long-drawn bellow from a boat on the river. In one street I saw two men walking – in a direction opposite to that in which we were going – but I dare not call them and make my explanation for fear of losing Kekewich. Apart from a cat, which at one time galloped alongside me for a few steps (and I was absurdly glad of its company), they were the only living creatures I saw. Kekewich must have known the whole district as well as he knew his own bedroom – we came to main roads only rapidly to cross them.

The moon had become very violet and I fancied that in the east the sky was already lightening; I suddenly observed against it anyway, over the house-tops, the black angular shapes of cranes. We had come to the river. I saw Kekewich at the end of the street we were in turn sharply left and vanish so instantaneously that I thought he must have gone into a house, and my heart sank. But when I came to the place of his disappearance I saw that he had gone through an archway – an archway low and echoing, its whitewashed interior lit crudely by a gas-lamp bracketed to the wall at its entrance. Through it I came into a little paved square, surrounded by houses. Kekewich was not there. I whirled round, expecting him to be by my side again, but the square was deserted. It was like a conjuring trick.

At the far side was a curiously domed structure with a light outside it shining on a notice board. I was so sure that I had lost Kekewich for ever that I ran, without any attempt at concealment, straight across the square and stopped under the illuminated notice, SHAPPING FOOT TUNNEL, it said, BY-LAWS. And then followed much small print which I did not stop to read. Somewhere in my brain the knowledge revived of the tunnel, which ran under the Thames (I recollected) for the convenience of pedestrians and was the first of its kind in the world: I even visualized the entry about it on the page of the revoltingly glossy book on London which Admiral Crowborough-Crow had once given me for Christmas.

Stone steps led up to the domed building. At the top of them was a notice:

TO THE LIFTS →
← WAY DOWN

There was no noise of the lifts: they surely could not be working at this hour of the morning. I turned left and found myself descending a broad staircase which spiralled down round the lift shaft. The walls were white-tiled and punctuated by gas lamps which sent out a harsh light with undertones of gloom. The staircase was divided from the shaft by a wire mesh; as I trod cautiously and silently down the steps I peered through the mesh and could see the staircase winding – endlessly it seemed – below. And then on the staircase, curiously foreshortened so that he seemed to be all bowler hat, I saw, with half-frightened relief (for I thought I had lost him and I half wanted to), Kekewich. He was hurrying now and looked as he sped from one step to the next, like a marionette. I moved down the spiral in time with him and so was able to keep him in view.

Suddenly, as though he were diving into water, his figure took a leap forward and fell head first down the steps and slithered out of my sight.

I stopped dead, and tried to hear what he was doing. I prayed that he had broken his neck. There was no sound except a dim, continuous roaring, as when a whorled shell is held to the ear, which came from the tunnel. I continued down the spiral.

He was nowhere on the steps. At the bottom of them, on the stone floor, in a corner, lay his bowler hat, still slightly rocking. In that place it seemed to me like a disturbing but incomprehensible symbol. I turned into the tunnel. Its round walls were lined with glazed white tiles; it dipped very gently, and then in the distance started rising again. I could not see the end of it; a little way past the beginning of the upward slope some sort of structure rose from the floor to the roof. Not fifty yards away, lying in the middle of the tunnel, like a bundle of old clothes, was Kekewich.

I slid back round the tunnel entrance. As I peered, Kekewich struggled to his feet, staggered to the tunnel wall, and, resting one shoulder against it, limped on so slowly and painfully that my stomach moved for him. Under the light of the tunnel – a white light like that of an operating theatre – I saw clearly his mane of hair, neither blond nor red nor grey, but the colour of dried, diluted blood. I waited for a long time until he had reached the obstructions in the tunnel and had disappeared from sight; several times he fell, his hand scraping at the smooth walls, and once, for a few steps, he crawled on his hands and knees. I think in his fall he must have broken a bone; his progress was achieved not by a physical effort, but by an effort of will. It was terrible to watch.

I ran lightly along the tunnel until I came up to the obstructions. I do not know what they were – perhaps vents or part of the air-conditioning machinery: they were three brick pillars placed close together. I edged past them and the final part of the tunnel came into view. The stone floor rose gently; the gleaming walls, obeying the laws of perspective, narrowed away in the distance. But the limping, crawling figure had utterly vanished.

I ran desperately some way up the slope before I realized what had happened. And then I turned and looked fearfully at the three pillars. There was nothing for it but to return to them. My feet took me slowly back. Between the first and the second pillar there was nothing. Between the second and third, wedged upright in the aperture to which the tunnel lights could not entirely penetrate, Kekewich stood looking at me.

*

He was standing, leant against a pillar, like a stork, on one leg; the other was bent, the knee against the opposite pillar. His face was livid, and across his high, sweating forehead was a black streak, no doubt acquired during his passage through the coal cellar, which made him, in a horrible way, look both doomed and ridiculous. A revolver dangled from his right hand.

He said: 'Come here.'

I could have got away. I could have doubled back round the pillars and I am sure he could not have followed me. But I stayed. As I saw him leaning there, it seemed to me that I understood him as though I had known him all my life: I saw his littered office, his awful clerks; I saw him coming up from the lavatory at the station with a cigar in his mouth; I saw his futile and involuntary gesture of concealment when Ben had taken me in to him at Savage's house.

'I have broken my ankle, I think,' he said.

There were no words with which I could reply to him. I stood and waited for the end of it all.

'The police could easily have been evaded,' he said. 'It was you they followed tonight.'

I shook my head. 'Brilliant told them.' My voice was dry and cracked.

'Brilliant dare not tell them. It was you we did not allow for. A boy. Why did you' – he paused and groaned – 'come into it? Why?'

I did not answer him. Our voices reverberated strangely round the curved roof of the tunnel. Above us floated boats and fish and weeds.

'You would say that the mistake was made when I killed Preece, wouldn't you? That was the tiny crack which started the whole . . .'

His voice trailed away. His white face was not facing me at all. He was staring at the bricks a few inches away from his eyes.

'The mistake was made years ago,' he said. 'When you could not have been born.'

Very faintly the sound of footsteps was carried to us by the trapped air in the tunnel. But I dare not turn my head to look. I think he heard them, because he turned his head towards me and started speaking very quickly.

'You will remember this, won't you? You will remember Kekewich in the tunnel? I will make you remember it all your life, you little –'

He raised the revolver. I felt – I think I could see – bands of blood suddenly across my eyelids. He raised his other hand and held the revolver with that, too. His sleeve was dusty from his fall. He opened his little mouth and put the muzzle of the gun in it. The enormous sound of the explosion went rolling for long seconds about the tunnel. When I could see again Kekewich was still standing there, his eyes still regarding me, but about the bottom of his face there was a dreadful, clotted absence, at which I dare not be tempted to look. I turned from the pillars and ran towards the innocent sane person wearing a cap and carrying an attaché case who now stood dubiously in the middle of the tunnel; ran as though he held a light for me in the middle of a dark, childish terror.

EPILOGUE: TUESDAY, 25 *September*

I KNOCKED on the baize-covered door of Mr Waggon's study. His light tenor voice said: 'Come in.' When I was inside the room he said: 'Ah, French.'

'Hullo, sir,' I said.

His nose was hovering over the tea-table.

'Chocolate cake!' I exclaimed, dutifully.

He was very pleased. 'Yes,' he said, 'I thought it was rather a favourite of yours.' Then he glanced rather slyly into the hearth.

'And crumpets,' I said. 'And a fire!'

'I find in my old age that these September days grow rather chilly about five o'clock.'

'It's quite a feast, sir. Who else is coming?'

'No one.'

'Really, sir?'

'Not a soul.'

'You will ruin my condition for the match on Saturday, sir.'

'Nonsense, French. I always used to train on crumpets.'

'But not chocolate cake as well.'

'This is a special occasion, French.' He turned his back to me and arranged the cushion in his basket chair. 'I want to know all about your murder case.'

'Oh,' I said.

He turned round and I saw that he had his frank smile on his face. 'Do sit down, boy. Have the arm-chair with the side wings. Sit back. Relax. There! And now for the crumpets.'

While we munched he said: 'I've no need to tell you, French, that I'm an incurable old gossip. And there was so little in the newspapers.' He sighed and wiped the butter from his chin. 'I hear all the boys talking about it and I feel absolutely and irritatingly ignorant. You know, French, I do regard you as under an obligation to me – that was a frightful paper you turned in on *The Black Dwarf.*'

'I'm sorry about the holiday task, sir. I'm afraid I left it rather late – and then along came the murder.'

'I sometimes feel,' said my form master, sadly, 'that I shall never impart my affection for Scott to you chaps.'

'Don't think that, sir. I'm sure we all rather like Sir Walter.'

'You don't find him just the *least* bit dull?'

'Not the least. A good, solid, interesting novelist, sir, at worst; at best, wonderful, of course.'

'Well,' said Mr Waggon, 'perhaps you'll find time for *The Dwarf* during term.'

'I hope so, sir. I've a very special love for it.'

'Have you?' he asked, dubiously.

'Yes, sir. It was really *The Black Dwarf* which enabled me to solve the case.'

'How perfectly sweet and thrilling. Tell me precisely how it all came about. And have a piece of chocolate cake.'

I looked over the desk at the window – a desk, as Mr Waggon had many times impressed upon me, which had formerly belonged to Alfred Austin, a poet with whom an ancestor of Mr Waggon had been connected by marriage and for whom Mr Waggon had a good deal of admiration – and through the window across the rather shaggy lawns which merged almost imperceptibly into the playing fields, where pale goal-posts sprouted in a rather melancholy way. The sun was on its way down, hidden by some wet and ragged clouds, over the line of hedge which indicated the road from the sea. Faint, continuous cries of boys came wafting on the wind, which flapped the lanyard of the flagstaff incessantly. In the foreground a fat gull sat on the handle of the garden-roller. I pulled myself together and turned to Mr Waggon who, with his long nose that drooped at the ends and his lank grey hair and his head on one side, looked like a thin gull. I swallowed my cake, and then said: 'Well, sir, it all started . . .'

*

When I had finished there was a long silence. Outside, the light still came brightly from over the sea, but the room had become quite dark. The fire gave out a small red glow; over the fireplace the drawing by Burne-Jones and the photograph of Mr Waggon as Old Gobbo in an O.U.D.S. production of *The Merchant of Venice* could no longer be identified. Mr Waggon lit another Cypriot cigarette.

'Good lord,' he said. 'Good lord.'

There was another silence.

Then Mr Waggon said: 'He was dead, of course?'

'Dead as a door-nail. I sat in the tunnel-keeper's – or whatever he was – office until Toller came. Toller had caught Savage and Ben and Savage's daughter at the house and hadn't known what had become of me. And, what is more astonishing, hadn't known of Kekewich. So the private investigator had really put one over on the police. I was the king-pin of the whole affair. Had a great interview with a Superintendent at the Yard – and so on.'

'And how *had* the Inspector got on to Savage and – er – Ben?'

'Elshie had broken down at last. They finally charged him with Preece's murder, and then, when he saw he was in all probability going to be hanged, he spilled the beans about Wren Road and the forgery set-up. But not about Kekewich – he still daren't do that.'

'I'm afraid I have a great many questions. I'm rather dense when it comes to explanations – I always have to read the end of a thriller twice,' said Mr Waggon. 'Daren't?'

'Oh, dear,' I said. 'Haven't I made it clear, sir? You see it wasn't clear to me until the police got a sketchy outline of it out of Savage. Elshie was absolutely in Kekewich's power. Kekewich in his more prosperous days had owned some property in London – among other things a shop, which at one time Elshie had rented and run as a bookshop. When the business failed Elshie put a match to it. Kekewich had either caught him or discovered the truth, but had never prosecuted him.'

'I see,' said Mr Waggon. But his brow was still corrugated. 'And so?'

'And so either through carelessness or compulsion Elshie had allowed his fingerprints to be on the gun which killed Preece.

Kekewich never handled it directly. Toller thinks he held it in his gown when he fired it and then simply let it drop on the floor during the *fracas*. Kekewich had told Elshie to run out of court at the sound of the explosion – and, of course, Elshie had obeyed. Toller thinks the defence will be able to show that Elshie is insane – he is simple as well as depraved.'

'The defence?' said Mr Waggon. I tried not to look at him pityingly. It was hard to believe that two years ago I had thought him a monument of intellect.

'They've charged Savage and Ben and Elshie with forgery, of course, sir.'

'Oh yes,' said Mr Waggon. 'Naturally. Will you be a witness at the trial?'

'No, sir. Toller says he has enough evidence without me. Alas!'

'Well, you wouldn't want to miss school, would you, French?' said Mr Waggon, with heavy irony.

'Goodness, no, sir.'

Mr Waggon probed reflectively with his thumb into his large nostril, as was his habit: some of the more vulgar, younger boys called him 'Pick-a-nose'.

'You know, French,' he said, at last, 'it really was a high-class thriller, wasn't it? I think, myself, that I prefer something more simple – something by Francis Beeding, say. I have never been able to follow more complicated plots. Sometimes during the holidays my aged mother – a rabid film fan – prevails upon me to go with her to the cinema. Always we seem to see an American murder mystery, where the murderer turns out to be a person of dubious identity whose face has been seen throughout the film in the shadows, and whose strenuous activities have been, to me at least, of a disconcerting ambiguity.' Mr Waggon took out his leather cigarette case again. 'Enthralling as your narrative has been, French, I am not at all sure that I properly understand it. That instructive information at the beginning about – what were they called? – the Rent and Mortgage Interest Restrictions Acts: just precisely how – you will think me very dull – did they bear on the murder?'

'I *haven't* made it clear, sir. You should have interrupted me.

I'm sorry to say, sir, that the position under the Rent Acts was the key to the whole case.'

Mr Waggon sighed. 'I thought it might be.'

'In fact,' I went on, 'I should have guessed everything that time in Brown's office when his clerk mentioned the Savage conveyance to him. Savage, you see, after Preece's death, was buying 2 Wren Road from Mrs Preece. All the apparatus for counterfeiting five-pound notes had been set up in the cellars of the house, where the counterfeiters thought they would be undisturbed. Savage was the tenant and, under the Rent Acts, couldn't be removed, unless the landlord – that was Preece' (I was putting it for him in words of one syllable) 'wanted the house for his own occupation *and* could show that his was the harder case. I think at the beginning Preece really did want his house back. Toller thinks that he smelt a rat in the first place. In any case it seems clear that Preece eventually knew that something fishy was going on, was blackmailing Savage, and brought the action when he wanted more money which Savage (directed by Kekewich, of course) refused to pay. The counterfeiters defended and delayed the action, and only took the step of killing Preece when it became absolutely clear that he was going to get possession of the house and that they would have to move or give Preece what he wanted. From what Brilliant has let out it seems Kekewich had made several alternative plans for murdering Preece.'

'Stupid to do it in court, I should have thought,' said Mr Waggon.

'In a way, yes. Though there wasn't much risk of actual discovery there. Kekewich could time it at the moment of greatest gloom and confusion, and he had Brilliant for a blind. The whole plan was typical of Kekewich. All that the police have discovered about him goes to show it. His wife had divorced him years ago for cruelty. He had almost been struck off the Roll of Solicitors in 1932 for beating up a client. His financial affairs had become progressively ruinous.'

'It is becoming much clearer,' said Mr Waggon. 'I see now that the threatening letters which Preece received, signed "Elshie" – '

' – were probably Brilliant's own feeble attempts,' I interrupted, 'to hold Preece off from 2 Wren Road. Remember, Preece probably never knew about Kekewich, who regarded himself, obviously, as a sort of Professor Moriarty sitting invisible at the centre of the web, his filaments stretching out . . .'

'That reminds me,' said Mr Waggon, 'they stretched out, didn't they, to Westsea Racecourse –'

'And Checklock Racecourse, too, sir. And several others, not to mention greyhound racing tracks, from which the police are still receiving reports of bogus bank notes being passed. That bears all the marks of a Kekewich idea. It was ingenious but wasteful. Every horse, or dog in the race was backed with spurious money. One of them – I'm sorry if I'm rather obvious, sir – was bound to win, and the winnings were, of course, paid out in good money.'

'Most ingenious,' said Mr Waggon. 'I have often wondered how counterfeiters got rid of their counterfeits. When I happen to be given an Irish penny or something I always have the utmost difficulty in palming it off on to somone else.'

'Yes, sir,' I said, looking out of the window again. I was getting very hoarse. The sky over the hedge was assuming the colours of the sunset.

'How very curious and coincidental about the Scott novel,' said Mr Waggon, whose conversational powers were prodigious. 'The – er gang really did nickname Brilliant "Elshie" after Sir Walter's character?'

'Well,' I said, uneasily, 'not the gang, exactly. It was the girl – Savage's daughter, you know, sir. That is why the coincidence wasn't so remarkable after all. Schoolmistresses as well as schoolmasters, no doubt, wish their pupils to become acquainted with the masterpieces of English Literature.'

'You are pulling my leg, French,' said Mr Waggon, delightedly.

'Nothing further from my mind, sir.'

He sent a stream of smoke towards me that smelt of the back streets of Port Said. 'The girl,' he said. 'The girl. I had forgotten about her. She was not the least remarkable of the remarkable characters concerned in it all.'

'Yes, sir,' I said. I had told him as little as I could about Rhoda.

'And, really,' he went on, remorselessly, 'it was she, not those awful Acts of Parliament, who was the key to the whole case.'

'I thought you said you didn't understand it, sir.'

He giggled. 'If she hadn't interfered, hadn't too imaginatively kept you from poking into matters, the dwarf would have been shipped out of the country, the house sold to Savage and the whole thing remained unsolved.'

'Perhaps.'

'It is a wonder Kekewich didn't murder her,' remarked Mr Waggon. 'I think I should have done. How exasperating! But I don't get a clear picture of her at all from what you have told me, French. What was she like?'

In the few seconds before I answered him I thought that I, too, had no clear picture of her. Whenever I tried precisely to remember her the muscles of my throat started aching.

'I don't really know,' I heard myself saying. 'An unmemorable person. Monkey-like in appearance – and in mischievousness – and agility.'

'They didn't charge *her* with forgery, did they?' asked Mr Waggon.

I shook my head. 'Toller said something about having her brought up before the magistrates as a person – what was it? – a person needing care and attention. I think that meant she would be sent to what is called an approved school.'

'A sort of young ladies' Borstal,' suggested Mr Waggon.

'Yes,' I said. 'Yes.'

He stubbed out his cigarette in the hollowed piece of lava he had once brought back from Mount Vesuvius, and stretched. 'Well, that will be the last of her. The ends are tied up very neatly, French.'

The last of her. I thought of the nights I had spent at home after that terrible night when Kekewich had committed suicide; nights of wandering about my room and the house, avoiding my father, or escaping into the streets to pace the quietest I could find. It had been a relief to come back to school; and though at first school and my activities in it had seemed remote and ridiculous, I was finding them more and more tolerable. But they would never seem the same again to me. Once, when I was younger, I had watched Admiral Crowborough-Crow drinking beer; with the glass at his lips he took a mouthful and gulped, then another mouthful and a gulp and so on. It seemed to me a very fine and adult way of drinking. The next time I drank, I drank like it, and the next time. But when I thought I would try my *old* way of drinking again, I found I couldn't drink in any other than the Admiral's way. I couldn't even imagine how there was another way. So with my simple existence before the fifth of September. Henceforth I should always be this split person, and what was usually regarded as normal life – the Mr Waggons and the Ronnie Reeves – present itself (amusing and interesting as it might be) only as an interlude in the abnormal, the truly normal life of love and death.

The gull had long since flown away from the roller. The sun was down: the sky had arranged itself in streamers of grey, mauve, and duck-egg green. Among the low, darkening trees which lined the road to the sea I thought I saw a patch of vivid colour which could not be sky. It was only for a moment that I saw it – a velvety cyclamen shade that seemed to be moving towards the school. A great beating filled the chamber of my ribs. I stood up.

'No hurry, French,' said Mr Waggon. 'Sit down, boy. You've half the chocolate cake to finish.'

'No, thank you, sir.' I thought he could not fail to notice my trembling voice. 'I must go. I have an essay to do for Mr Hume tonight.'

'Ah,' said Mr Waggon, preparing to be malicious. 'And what striking subject has Mr Hume found for you to sharpen your wits on?'

I sidled towards the door. I had to get away, and quickly. 'How did England view the Continental revolutions of 1848, and why?'

'Tst,' said Mr Waggon. 'It is always revolution with Mr Hume. For him, the progress of history takes place on rivers of blood.'

'Yes, sir, but we make the necessary corrections.' I was aching with the desire to flee, with worry, and with the thought of happiness. My knees felt weak with trying to move without my feet. 'Well, sir, thank you very much indeed for tea.'

'The pleasure and the gratitude are all mine, French,' said Mr Waggon. 'My curiosity has been beautifully appeased. Mr Hume, now – '

I pretended not to hear his last three words, and, murmuring 'Good-bye', closed the baize-covered door firmly behind me. And then I ran out of school towards the road to the sea.

www.ingramcontent.com/pod-product-compliance
Ingram Content Group UK Ltd.
Pitfield, Milton Keynes, MK11 3LW, UK
UKHW031420100125
453365UK00004B/192

9 781960 241399